Louisa:
A Modern Faith Story

BETH TROY

READERS' PRAISE FOR *LOUISA*

"If you are looking for a fresh voice in Christian fiction, you are certain to find that in Beth Troy. Her unique still is 100% real. The characters are imperfect in the best way possible, making her stories all the more relatable to all readers. I cannot get enough!" – Randi Sampson, *A Modern Day Fairytale*

"The gift of not being able to set a book down is rare. And right now you hold that gift. Beth writes with such enjoyable suspense and subtle laugh-out-loud humor you'll be taking this book from room to room with you. She effortlessly captures the journey of a woman wading through the complexity of faith and the gift of being truly honest with oneself in spiritual growth. I loved every page." – Amy Seiffert, author of *Grace Looks Amazing On You* and *Chin Up*

"You'll be pulled in from the get-go with Beth Troy's unique, engaging, honest and witty writing. *Louisa* is a brilliant novel about a woman trying to figure out what it means to be a woman, daughter, sister, friend, and a Christian—how that fits into and applies to her messy life. No matter where you are in these roles, *Louisa* will make you think and cry and question and perhaps even seek a richer fuller life that satisfies your soul." – Laura L. Smith, best-selling author of *How Sweet the Sound.*

"This series is a must read for all new Christians! Well, actually everyone ..." – Jessica Baker, *A Baker's Perspective*

"Real faith. Real struggle. Real life. Beth Troy has penned a mesmerizing love story, an authentic spiritual awakening, and a compassionate and profound journey of one woman's search for belonging and purpose that is unmissable." – Rel Mollet, *Relz Reviewz*

"Speechless is how I felt after I read *Louisa*." – Ebos Aifuobhokhan

OTHER MODERN FAITH STORIES
BY BETH TROY

Lu.

ii

WHAT IS A MODERN FAITH STORY?

It's a story about how God is real and deals with real people.
It's a story of faith lived in real ways.
It's a story written in words real people use.

It doesn't moralize. It doesn't pretend.
It doesn't apologize, and it doesn't excuse.

It presents as plainly as possible what it means to be human and the
rescue we all have in Jesus Christ.

For the girls who have found but are wondering where they fit –
this one's for you

CHAPTER 1: LU

At least the trees were cooperating with my plan.

I'd plotted the scene in my mind — the stillness of the cemetery, the reverence of my approach, the flowers in my hand. Even after eight hours of thinking time on yesterday's drive home, I hadn't been able to script what I'd say when I got here. I figured I'd find the words when I needed them.

In retrospect, I should have nixed the flowers. The grocery's flower department opens at 9:00 on Sundays. Church starts at 9:30, which is why I planned to buy the daisies yesterday, but yesterday hadn't worked, either.

I blamed this on my family, who hadn't rehearsed their parts in my surprise return. It started with them being home when I arrived yesterday afternoon, but when I reached for the doorknob, no one turned it from the inside.

"Hello?" I called, poking my neck from the vestibule. I looked left. I looked right. Nothing.

I wandered the hallway, greeting the empty family room, dining room, and kitchen. I looked through the screen door to the deck and backyard. When I didn't see anyone, I climbed to the second floor, and then to my attic bedroom in case they were hiding under the bed.

I started unpacking, ready and wanting to be interrupted any minute, but my parents didn't come home until dinner. They had my three little nieces in tow, which didn't leave room for more than a surprised look and then a grateful one. It wasn't until after we'd divvied the hot dogs, potato chips, and apple slices that my parents got around to asking why I was home, but by then my nieces' parents had arrived from next door – my best friend, Gracie, and my brother, Ted.

"Back again, Lu-ser?" Ted asked and laughed, despite Gracie's warning look.

His question brought all eyes to me, giving me the attention I'd wanted three hours ago. I opened my mouth to answer, but the diversity of my audience stumped me. How I'd tell the story to my parents was different than what I'd share with Gracie. As for my nieces, I'd planned on reappearing in their lives with snow globes of the Empire State Building and without a backstory.

I closed my mouth, leaving them to fill in the blanks.

"John?" Mom asked, referring to my ex-boyfriend in New York. "He cheated on you again?"

I shook my head, and Gracie's eyes widened. She put her hand to her mouth and whispered, "Oh no, you didn't come back because I told you about …"

I tried to stop her sentence with another headshake, but she'd said too much.

"You came back for Jackson!" Ted shouted before he started laughing at me for the second time in a minute. Not a record, but still not welcome. "I hate to tell you Lu-ser, but that's over …"

Dad cut him off with a look. Caroline, my oldest niece at nine-years-old, continued instead.

"Have you seen his new girlfriend, Aunt Lu? She's so pretty with blonde curls and …"

"Quiet."

I held up my hand, which shut their mouths, but not their eyes. Those told me I was pathetic.

"I didn't come back for Jackson."

And a liar.

"I didn't!"

I looked around, pleading with someone, anyone to believe me. No one did – not even Dad, who's not supposed to vote in Lu Pity Polls, or my niece, Holly, who's three years old and supposed to think I'm a hero. Or maybe I was misinterpreting why she'd crumpled to the floor and buried her face in her hands.

Nothing I said held any sway the rest of the night, and I was more determined than ever to visit Grandma Pat's grave the next morning. I set my alarm in plenty of time to get ready and get to the grocery when it opened. Would I also pick up Nana Bea on the way, Mom asked as I made my coffee? If I said no, she'd ask why. So, I said yes.

Her house was one turn off my route – at most, a few extra minutes.

"Jackson is dating someone, Lu," she offered as a greeting.

I ignored her words, like how I now tried to ignore she was the third wheel on my pilgrimage. Nana stayed in the car as I scrambled to the grave, clutching a daisy bouquet with my right hand. Leave it to Grandma to purchase her plot at the top of the hill.

When I paused to breathe, I noticed the trees. They, in their spring hybrid of half-leaf, half-blossom, were on point, as was the breeze that caressed my face before catching pink and white blooms in a whirlwind. I spent a minute I didn't have watching the blossoms twirl down, decorating Grandma Pat's tombstone in a way her creative eye would have appreciated.

I knelt to pick one up, rubbing the silky petal between my thumb and forefinger. A lot had happened in New York, and Grandma Pat would appreciate any way I'd tell it. I stood back up.

Out with it, I could hear her say. *Say what you came to say.*

But I'd never said something like this before, and the only memories that came to mind were from high school when normal kids would leave for a youth retreat on Friday and return strange on Monday.

I gave Jesus my heart. I prayed the prayer.

I couldn't talk like that, not even to a grave in an empty cemetery.

Nana honked. I had 30 seconds. Why was I here? Not because I thought Grandma Pat was sitting around in glory, waiting for me to awkwardly recount what she probably already knew.

And with that thought, I realized I didn't need to say anything at all.

I cleared my throat.

"So, we'll talk later – after church. And no, I'm not going there because of Jackson. You were wrong about him. He didn't wait for me."

I looked at her tombstone: a small gray rectangle flush with the grass, nondescript but for her name and one verse.

Whoever drinks the water I give him will never thirst. Indeed, the water I give him will become a spring of water welling up to eternal life – John 4:14.

I knelt again, my right hand catching the bottom corner of the tombstone between my thumb and pointer finger. If I traced these words would I find mine?

"You were wrong about Jackson. But you were right about everything else."

It wasn't until I opened the car door that I noticed I was still holding the daisies. Nana raised her eyebrows, and I handed her the bouquet without a word.

CHAPTER 2: LU

The last time I'd walked into this church was for Grandma Pat's funeral. It was a beautiful space, a medley of windows and natural wood that gave the illusion of being more outside than in. My brother designed it. My father built it. I'd never intended to come back.

I routed Nana to my family as the congregation stood to sing. Performance anxiety hit me. I wanted to sing, but given my family's assumption of why I'd returned, plus the rest of the church knowing only the Lu who'd left, singing didn't feel like an option today.

I closed my eyes instead – a handy childhood trick. Maybe the darkness that masked the crowd could also hide one half of me from the other. I wanted to be here; I wanted to run from here. I directed my mind to buoy the first thought and ignore the second.

Stay here. Be here.

The first hymn was background noise. The second broke through my chant with lyrics I could dust from memory. I whispered them, giving my body something to do other than fold my hands into new shapes.

My God, my portion, and my love,
My everlasting All,
I've none but thee in heaven above

The verses settled and unsettled me. God, the one and only, and the choice I'd made. Everything had changed for me my last night in New York, and the next step, as best as I understood it, was to return home to Dunlap's Creek. Why had I thought my new belief would go in front of me like a public service announcement, excusing me from having to explain anything? Why had I thought my family would see something different about me or this return? I'd pulled the same move last year. There was no reason for them or anyone else in this church to see a change.

The reality was simple and hard. Home was waiting for me with the mess I'd left, and I had a lot of explaining to do.

I opened my eyes, and Jackson took the stage.

I'd already wasted too much time pretending he didn't affect me. I stared at him without break, his voice running over my senses.

The present mixed with memory – first, to the last sermon I'd heard Jackson preach. *Jesus is the answer. Jesus is the conclusion of the matter. God is here for you. God can save you. Do you believe that?*

I answered his question with the one that had stopped me every time.

Save me from what?

It would take another four months for me to answer it. It started when I lost my job that next day and continued through Grandma Pat's funeral a few weeks later. Then my ex-boyfriend, John, came back. He asked for a second chance, and I said yes. I guess it was my decision, but it felt inevitable. I went back to New York City. It was easily done so long as I avoided the one person who could keep me here.

Stay, Jackson had said.

Stay with you? I'd countered.

He didn't answer, I left for New York, and four months later I was back with the answer. *Yes. I do believe God saved me. But it's a little late for you and me.*

I looked down, surprised to see I'd been taking notes and wondered what my hand had been up to while my mind rewound.

I looked at my family, sitting to my left along the length of the pew, their eyes trained forward. I understood their doubt about why I was back, but they were wrong. I hadn't returned to reclaim Jackson. I returned to reclaim my life.

But I wanted to be with Jackson all the same.

His eyes found mine. I made no move – no move to mask my thought. This I held out to him, like an offering.

He was close to finishing his sermon, but he stopped when he saw me. In his pause I could see I'd ordered my return all wrong. I should have gone to see him first.

It was going to be a complicated apology.

A cough to the left broke our stare and Jackson picked up where he stopped. Three questions, and he was finished. He took a seat. We stood to sing. I kept my eyes open this time. When the song ended, I looked at Gracie.

What do I do now? I silently asked.

She looked to Jackson and back at me.

I have no idea, her shrug said.

There? I pointed to the exit. *Or there?* I pointed to the stage.

She shrugged again, and I grabbed my purse, intending to follow my family out and deal with all of this later, but Nana Bea put her hand on my arm.

"Retreat now, and you will keep doing it."

She was right. I headed forward.

Forward movement was a slow progression of welcome back conversations with people on their way out. How was the city? Was I back for good or a visit? Was I going to write again for *The Daily*? All innocuous, unanswerable questions, but I did the best I could, treading the baseline of politeness while my nervousness escalated.

It took forever, but Jackson was standing in front of me before I was ready. My breath caught again.

"Back for a visit," he said.

The old Jackson would have smiled. He would have asked instead of presumed. But these were minor problems compared to his tone. It wasn't anger.

It was empty.

I shook my head, and his expression didn't change. There was a lot to say, and the faster I said it, the better. I just needed an hour first to think about how to do that.

"New York didn't work out," he said – his second observation.

"It did. I didn't work out in it."

He nodded and started to turn away, but I reached for his arm. He looked at my hand and then at me. He didn't move.

That's when I noticed the woman beside him. She was pretty and with golden curls, but Caroline had left out what a friendly smile the woman had. Her face welcomed it, like she was the type to smile more often than not.

I removed my hand as she extended hers to greet me. Jackson stepped back so we could step toward each other.

"Louisa, this is Rebecca, my girlfriend. She teaches at the elementary school. Rebecca, this is Louisa ..." He paused, unsure of how to classify me. I empathized. What we were had never been certain, though I'd said "friends" often enough.

But what Jackson landed on was nothing at all.

"Louisa is from Dunlap's Creek, and her family goes to church here. Tell them I said hello, Louisa."

Jackson put his hand on Rebecca's back to greet the people behind me, and I was dismissed. I tried to mask the dunce cap I felt like I was wearing with fake smiles and nods to the straggling parishioners, hoping I'd make it to my car before I scream-cried.

I didn't see Jackson's father until he greeted me.

"Hello, Lu," he said with a kind smile. I'd always been a little scared of Paul Cleary, who was my pastor growing up. Right now, he was way less scary than his son. I stopped to shake his hand.

"It's nice to see you," he continued. "Are you going to be around for a while?"

"I think so."

"How about you come to my office Tuesday morning? I have a project that might interest you for the church's 50th anniversary celebration."

"Oh, I don't plan events anymore."

"It's more on the writing side of things. A book of sorts, to document the church's history."

I shook my head for a lot of reasons, the main one seeing rejection as the fastest way out of here, but he put his hand on my shoulder and smiled again.

"Would you consider it?"

Which is how my shake turned to a nod because out of all the people welcoming me back to our small town, I'd found one to consider me.

CHAPTER 3: JACKSON

I saw Louisa's eyes, and then I saw her as she'd been the morning she told me she'd smashed her phone with a hammer. Who hammers her phone to avoid an ex-boyfriend and then talks about it like it's just another day?

But that's Louisa. I had a dozen more memories like it – of her doing and saying what most people only think – but her eyes this morning took me to that morning last summer when we worked her grandma's pierogie stand at the Farmer's Market. I took charge of sales, and she stayed behind the skillet, happy for a reason to keep her eyes down. She was trying to make herself invisible, but it was the first time I kept looking at her. Or at least the first time I noticed I was.

I have no idea how the conversation made its way to hammered phones, but I remember laughing. I remember how she kept a straight face, but her eyes told a different story. There was a light in the brown that hinted maybe she was in the moment with me instead of the distant place her mind often went.

Her eyes told the same story this morning. I locked into her gaze like a habit – that habit of letting my eyes speak what my words couldn't. It'd been months, but I looked at Louisa now like I'd been expecting her any minute.

I saw her and my mouth shut, my mind too far back to know what came next. A cough from somewhere in the congregation broke into the quiet, fast-forwarding me from that man last summer, who didn't know any better, to now. I looked at my notes and saw I was three questions from finishing. I asked them out loud to the congregation and left the stage for the final hymn.

It would be at least another hour before I got out of here, and the five minutes before we finished the hymn wasn't enough time for me to process anything.

The line of people to talk with after church queued like any other Sunday. Rebecca joined me, and we greeted people together. It was all normal except for how I felt. I was almost relieved when Louisa stood in front of me. The faster I moved through this, the better.

"Back for a visit," I said, hoping that was the case.

Something in her eyes shifted before she shook her head. I waited for her to say something else, and when she didn't, I tried again.

"New York didn't work out."

Another shift. "It did. I just didn't work out in it."

She followed her statement with more silence – our familiar pattern of me drawing her out and her drawing me in. I was about to move to the next person in line when I felt her hand on my arm. I looked from her hand to her face, and my eyes took her in while my brain told me to stop. So much about Louisa was unchanged.

In the end, it was Rebecca's hand that removed Louisa's from my arm. As they shook hands, I realized Rebecca was one of the few people at church who didn't know Louisa.

"Rebecca, this is Louisa …" I paused, unsure of how to label our relationship. Rebecca was easy – girlfriend. And Louisa was … Louisa and I weren't anything.

I finished the introduction and moved on, probably too quickly. I was relieved for it to be over. I looked at Rebecca. Her eyes asked a question. One more conversation, I thought. And then it would be over.

CHAPTER 4: LU

"It doesn't sound all that bad," Gracie concluded.

"What do you mean it doesn't sound all that bad? Because Jackson didn't throw me out of church?"

We prepped Sunday supper – frozen meatballs, jarred tomato sauce, boxed pasta, frozen garlic bread, and bagged Caesar salad. It was the opposite of what Grandma Pat had cooked for us on a daily basis, not to mention all the homemade extras she'd make on Sundays. But it was the best Mom, Gracie, and I could do.

Nana, as always, sat at the table doing nothing. She was here for the commentary.

"I'm proud of Lu for taking a stand," she said.

I snorted as I set the meatballs and sauce to simmer on the stove.

"I wouldn't say I took a stand, Nana."

"You dealt with it. You could have left."

"True, but the only thing I accomplished was meeting 'Rebecca.'"

"Why the air quotes? That's her name." Gracie laughed.

"Well, she looks like she belongs in a storybook."

"He's up to his old pattern – playing it safe," Nana said.

"Can you blame him?" Mom asked.

"Whose side are you on?" I glared. "And what's this about Rebecca working at the elementary school? You could have told me you work with her."

Mom ignored me, but Nana continued. "I don't see what he's in a snit about. You weren't beholden to him when you went back to New York. In my day, there wasn't a deal until the ring was on the finger."

"I'll make sure to tell Jackson that after church next Sunday." I leaned my forehead against my arms on the counter. "What a mess."

"What did you expect, honey?" Mom asked, too busy rummaging in the utensil drawer to witness my second glare of the day. I took the forks and knives from her and started setting the table.

"I don't know. I didn't expect Jackson to be so ..." I paused, replaying the moment. Whatever I'd felt when he first saw me and paused was gone by the time I got to him after church. He was calm, polite, and far from me.

"You're right," I said to Nana as I put a fork and knife in front of her. "There wasn't a ring on my finger. Jackson and I weren't more than friends, but he deserved more than me leaving for New York with John and no explanation. Today, I wanted to ..."

I trailed off again, still unsure how to say this.

"What?" Mom asked, following me around the table with plates.

The real reason stuck in my mouth like cotton. I settled for Option B.

"I wanted to apologize."

My cop-out landed like the *duh* it was. I heard it in their silence.

"You would have saved yourself a world of trouble if you'd picked up the phone to apologize to Jackson."

"For what?" Ted asked, entering the dining room at the wrong time with the girls and Dad.

"For leaving," Mom said.

"Too little, too late if you ask me."

"I didn't ask you," I shouted. And then I chucked a meatball at him because ... I don't know. It was something to do. He caught the meatball, popped it in his mouth and wiggled his eyebrows to dare me for another round.

He'd started it, but of course, Mom blamed me.

"Lu! We do not throw meatballs in the house!"

Gracie took my side.

"Ted, you're sleeping on the couch if you bug Lu again," she warned before sitting with a sigh. She was very pregnant. "Not that you'd mind. I feel ready to burst."

And with that, dinner moved to another topic, bringing temporary reprieve while extending the inevitable. At some point, I had to find words to articulate the change that was apparent only to me, or at least so I thought until I heard a knock on my bedroom door later that evening.

It was Gracie, carrying two mugs of hot chocolate.

"How much longer until the baby comes?" I asked as she sat next to me on the bed.

"Too long."

"I'm glad I made it back."

"I'm glad you're back," she said.

"You mean that?"

"Of course I do." She squeezed my hand. "Now tell me what happened."

I took a sip, welcoming the bitter taste of the dark chocolate, but wishing it brought some clarity with it. I shrugged.

"I think that's my problem. I don't know how to talk about what happened."

"With John?"

I took another sip. "John and other things."

"You started to tell us before dinner."

"Can you blame me for stopping? I spent so much time in New York missing everyone, but the family seems to assume nothing happened to me between then and now."

"Are you any different with us? It's been hard, Lu. After you came back last summer, we were a big family all the time. Then Grandma Pat died, and Nana Bea moved back to her house. You left for New York with John, and we haven't talked to Jackson – not really – since you left. Everything shifted. We want you home but give it time. You have time."

She looked at me, alarmed. "You aren't going anywhere, right?"

Gracie was my best friend since girlhood, and my sister-in-law for the last eight years. She was honest and kind, more committed to our family than I'd ever been. It took courage to meet her eyes.

"Would you believe me if I told you I was here to stay?"

We'd fought often enough through the years, but our fight before I'd returned to New York was the worst. I'd promised to stick around through the birth of baby #4, but took it back when everything fell apart. Gracie had forgiven me, and we'd talked almost every day I was gone.

She nodded. "Of course I believe you, and I trust whatever happened that was big enough to bring you back here is big enough to keep you here, even though it's awkward right now. You'll be able to talk about it when it's time."

She put her mug and mine on the nightstand and turned to me, holding both of my hands.

"Lu, I'm sorry about Jackson."

That was all I needed to cry. Dealing with my feelings for Jackson had been hard enough. I hadn't ever talked about them, but with Gracie I didn't have to. She knew that what started as a friendship hadn't ended that way, which is why she'd called me in New York to tell me Jackson was with someone – a someone I never could have been, at least not when I left.

I cried and cried while she handed me fresh tissues at a steady clip across her pregnant belly. When I finished, she hugged me and left without a word, leaving both mugs behind in case I needed a double.

I left them on the nightstand and walked to the nearest dormer window. I heaved the leaded window open, bracing it with an old dictionary, then cupped the air with my hands and brought it to my nose. Rain was coming. It'd make my room spring fresh within the hour. I was going to take longer.

I returned to my bed and my mug, looking around as I took a sip. I pointed to the space beyond the foot of my bed. That was where Jackson stood, when he asked me to stay. I moved my finger ten degrees to the right. That was where I'd stood when I'd asked whether that meant staying with him. He didn't answer, and instead of pressing further, I'd asked him to leave. The distance had felt huge, and if I couldn't take those three steps to bridge it then, what hope was there now?

I reached into my back pocket and pulled out my notes from church. I followed the page with my finger, surprised at how well I'd outlined Genesis 12. *God calls Abraham as father of a new nation. Abraham is old and childless. Why him? It has nothing to do with him. It's about God. God's grace and love to redeem one and through one, to redeem all.*

Abraham got to leave his hometown, his house, and his people. He got to go to a new place.

I closed my eyes and leaned my head against the pillows, spreading my hands in defeat.

"Why did you bring me back?"

CHAPTER 5: LU

I hoped I wouldn't run into Jackson again at church when I met with his dad on Tuesday morning, unless of course I could push out the words this time.

Our church had two buildings – the new chapel out of town that held Sunday services and the original building in the center of town that held everything else a church does. The core of the old building was a rectangular chapel the church had bought when it first started. In the 50 years since, it had been added onto in strange ways. Dunlap's Creek is a small town, but home to several old churches that are pretty enough to draw out-of-towners for weddings, which had made for a lot of choices when I was covering the wedding beat for *The Daily* last year.

Our old church building was not one of those churches, but it would be, if my dad's enthusiasm over the blueprints at breakfast signaled anything. He'd moved his finger around the diagrams as he explained how they were making large spaces feel smaller and the small spaces feel larger. It felt like an IQ test of folded paper and dots. I would have to figure it out when I got there.

The front door opened into demolition – a maze of coated plastic sheeting, spotlights, and shadows of people with nail guns and saws. I picked my way forward, stepping over extension cords and remnants of what used to be the dropped ceiling. The farther I walked, the more the church resembled something familiar. Walls replaced tarps, and I spied a sign with labels and arrows. I moved down the hall and two rights to the office. It opened to a small sitting area untouched by the construction.

"Hey, Lu," the cheerful voice of the receptionist greeted me.

I looked at the brass nameplate on her desk.

"Hello … Betty. Is Pastor Cleary in?"

She nodded and gestured for me to follow her as she knocked on the closed door to the right of the seating area. A moment later, I sat across from Jackson's dad with Betty handing me a Styrofoam cup of coffee. I'd already had two cups from my French press at home, but she offered this with such a bright smile that I took it. When she didn't move, I sipped, covering my grimace with a return smile and nod. It tasted like pollution.

Betty left, closing the door behind her. I was prepared for an uncomfortable conversation, ending with me rejecting Pastor Cleary's job offer. Then something caught my eye – the April edition of *NYNY*, the magazine I'd written for in New York.

"Where did you get this?" I asked as I popped out of my seat to grab it. The magazine was a reminder my time there hadn't been a complete waste.

"Your nana, Bea, brought it into the office a couple weeks ago. Did you enjoy writing for the magazine?" he asked, resuming his seat behind the desk.

"Yes. Completely."

I stopped and looked down, attempting to put words to a sense of purpose I still barely understood. I opened to the center spread of the story I'd written on New York's social entrepreneurship scene.

"I've always liked to write, but before this, I did it for me. I liked to see my byline on the page, and the story was a way to do that. But these people starting businesses for the sole purpose of benefitting others? That's amazing. I felt honored they'd make time for me. The writing was less about me and became more a way I could help."

"I could tell it suited you," he said. "Since you're back, I thought you might be interested in another writing project. We're celebrating the church's 50th anniversary in two months, and I'd like for you to write a short history of the church and its people, which is another way of saying I'd like for you to dig through boxes of documents and make sense of them. We'll pay you, of course."

I hadn't given one thought to how I was going to pass my time, let alone make a living. Granted I'd been back less than three days, but another twelve hours, week, or month wasn't going to change the job economy of Dunlap's Creek. Still, I hesitated.

Pastor Cleary continued.

"This would be your project. I'm happy to answer any questions you might have along the way. Church history is a web of connections, and I think I have enough memory left to help you clarify who's who. But I'll leave the job of storytelling to you. We could pay you a thousand dollars."

I had a little over $8,000 in my account, thanks to the generosity of my parents, who had charged minimal rent when I returned home last year, and John, who had charged me nothing during my few months in New York. I'd never earned much, and I was frugal by nature, but if I was ever going to live on my own, I'd want more in my savings. This offer gave me money and time to figure that out.

"I'll do it. Thank you, Pastor Cleary."

"Paul," he corrected.

I made a face, and he laughed.

"Do you call Jackson 'Pastor Cleary?'"

I almost snorted coffee out of my nose. "No."

"Paul it is then."

He smiled and stood as the door opened behind me.

It was Jackson holding a box.

"Okay, Dad. This is the first of about a thousand. Where do you …" and then he trailed off, having looked from the box to me. I smiled, my reflexes lagging behind reality. Jackson's neutral smile tamped them down, though.

"Hello, Louisa. I'm sorry for interrupting."

He was so polite. I looked at his dad, but Paul's face didn't reflect the look I'm sure was playing all over mine. Jackson finished his question.

"Where do you want me to take these, Dad?"

Paul looked at me. "There are a lot of boxes, more than you'd want to haul back and forth from the church to your house. It's a mess here with all of the construction, but you could use the storage area in the basement."

"How about I start loading these in your car, Louisa?" Jackson asked.

Like his smile, it was polite, but the question felt more like a takeover. It deferred a decision that would normally be easy for me to make. Home was quiet, at least during the day, and home wasn't church. But wasn't church something I was supposed to start getting used to? This project would help me get involved. I didn't need to work from here, too. Working from home might make a good reprieve.

I was about to tell Jackson to take the boxes to my car, but he forced me the other way.

"I can put the box in your car right now, Louisa. I'm sure you'd prefer to do this at home."

Really? He was sure of what I'd prefer. *I'd prefer you look at me, not through me. I'd prefer you remember me. I'd prefer to know whether everything I felt about us had been all in my head.*

I looked at Jackson, and he looked at me.

"And why is that?" I asked after I sipped my coffee to make him wait.

"Why is what?"

"That you're sure I'd prefer to do this at home."

"The church is a mess."

"Mess doesn't bother me."

"Since when would you prefer to be at church instead of home?"

He had me there, and he knew it.

I took another sip of this now fascinating cup of coffee. "I'm getting used to churches."

"Really?"

"New York was filled with them," I said, mimicking his didactic tone.

"Then it's all settled," Paul interjected. We looked at him and then at each other. Nothing was settled. I was warming to the fight, and the look on Jackson's face said he had a lot more to say, too.

"Jackson, go ahead and take Lu to the storage room. Lu, it's a bit dark, but the space is big enough for you to unpack all of the history and see what you have to work with. Thanks for taking this on."

And with that, we were dismissed.

I smiled at Betty as I followed Jackson out of the church office. The sounds of construction punctuated our otherwise silent walk down the hall and basement stairs, which emptied into a colorful hallway of kids' Sunday school classrooms. The scene hadn't changed much from my childhood; I could still taste the lukewarm grape juice. We went through two more sets of double doors until we landed at the part of the basement that looked every bit cellar. No primary colors, just gray cinder block walls and a solitary light bulb in the middle of the ceiling. Surely this was the room where they filmed every horror movie ever.

"Great mountain to die on, Lu," I muttered to myself.

"What's that?" Jackson asked, putting the box down.

I nodded toward the lone ceiling light.

"If you insist on working here, I'll bring down more lights for you."

"Jackson, I'm not insisting ..."

His look interrupted me. It didn't see through me. And, it wasn't polite.

"Yes, you are."

This was my opening to the five minutes I claimed I wanted. I opened my mouth to take it, but then said, "I don't want to bother you. I'll bring a light from home."

I closed my eyes like the coward I was, and when I opened them again, Jackson was gone. I sighed, leaning against the cold wall, shaking my head back and forth a couple times before picking up where I left off.

"It might interest you to know I've changed," I said to his vanished self. I held up the Styrofoam as evidence. "I drink crap church coffee now. That's a big deal, right?"

His ghost didn't respond to the revelation, so I toasted the box at my feet, tossing the sludge back in one shot before unpacking.

CHAPTER 6: JACKSON

I returned to my dad's office and shut the door behind me.

"Why Louisa, Dad?"

"She's a great writer, and she's willing. It's thankless work. How many boxes do you think are down there?"

I ignored his question.

"Why Louisa, Dad?"

"Have you seen this?"

He pushed an open magazine toward me. I looked down and saw an article with her name on it.

"Dad. When Louisa left, she left. It wouldn't have been helpful, to either of us, to keep track of her." I walked to the window, rubbing the back of my neck. "I want to know why, out of all the people in this town, you asked her to do this?"

We looked at each other through the reflection in the glass.

"Why not?"

"I can't have a repeat of last year."

"This isn't about you. It's about her."

I shook my head and turned to face him. "And you think you know Louisa?"

"Of course not, but I saw her on Sunday – before you did." So, he'd noticed the break in my sermon. "Why do you think she's back?"

"I don't know."

"She was doing well for herself. She talked about her work in New York at great length while she was here. It seemed like she found a part of herself there. Why would she give up this," he tapped the magazine, "to come back here?"

"I don't care."

"You spent most of last year with her. We didn't have a conversation without you bringing her up. Now she's back, and you say you don't know why and don't care. That isn't like you, Jackson."

I had come in here to get my dad to answer me, but he'd cornered me, and with such ease I wondered how long he'd been wanting to talk with me about this. He'd asked me about Louisa once, right after she left for New York. I told him I would talk to him was when I was ready. I never had.

I still wasn't sure how much I wanted to say or how much he wanted to hear. I put my hands in my pockets and leaned against the window ledge.

"The last time I talked to Louisa, she accused me of turning her into a project."

"Meaning?"

"Meaning, I wanted her to believe in God more than I cared about her."

"Was it true?"

I took a breath.

"No. I just wanted her."

We didn't say anything for several seconds. His eyes were understanding, but not because he'd experienced anything like this. He'd met my mom in elementary school. Theirs was the example I'd chased in my marriage to Kate. Which ended in divorce.

I took my hands out of my pockets and spread them in the helplessness I still felt about all of it.

"It didn't start that way. When I came back to town after my divorce, it was uncomfortable. A divorced pastor – a pastor's divorced son – no one wants to talk about that, at least not to me. People were nice enough, but everything was surface level. You and I talked about it after I accepted the position. I knew it would take time. Still, it was hard.

"And then I went to a baseball game one afternoon, and there was Louisa Sokolowski sitting next to me. It'd been years since I'd seen her, but I knew who she was. I don't think she would have ever looked up from the book she was reading, if it weren't for the kiss cam. Whoever was operating it was having a good time. For all I cared, the camera could zoom in and out from us for the rest of the game, but it bothered Louisa."

"Kiss me," she'd said.

"What?" It seemed like an odd ask for a woman who hadn't noticed me and like a bad move for a pastor people weren't sure about.

"The camera's not going anywhere, and I don't like being the main attraction."

"Do you think I do, Louisa?"

"Lu," she corrected. She looked at me, and I saw something familiar in her eyes. Loneliness.

"I kissed her hand, the camera went away, and she ignored me for the rest of the game. I ran into her at a wedding the next weekend, and then her grandma invited me to dinner. You saw it happen, Dad. We became friends. To other people in this town, I was the divorced pastor, but not to Louisa because it wasn't something she cared about. She didn't believe in God, and I didn't need to be her pastor. She wouldn't have put up with it, anyway. And on top of that …"

The memory of the smashed phone again. Of us playing cornhole in her parents' backyard. All the times she tried to force me to drink coffee. The time she called my preaching of Ecclesiastes self-flagellation. How she looked last Thanksgiving and how it felt to hold her before her grandma's funeral. I could see the tears running down her face and feel them on my fingers as I wiped them away. I could hear myself whispering to her. I am here for you.

I took another breath. "On top of that, she's Louisa. I've never met anyone like her. And that's what I told her before I asked her to stay."

"To stay with you?" Dad asked.

I swallowed. This was the hardest part – the part I'd run through my mind over and over in the weeks after she left.

"No, just to stay. I didn't offer anything. I can't be with someone who doesn't believe in God. It'd never work. I know this, but I wanted to be with her anyway. I asked her to stay. Louisa was the one to do the right thing and cut off whatever we had."

"And after that?"

I turned back to the window. This is where my confession stopped. My dad didn't need to hear about the first week after Louisa left. The anger, first, at her for leaving without another word or thought for me, and then, at me for putting myself in this position. That's when I realized how far in I was. I'd talked about God with her – answered her questions, countered her arguments – but somewhere along the way, I didn't just want her to believe in God. I wanted her to believe in God because it was the way I could be with her, a point she'd pressed the last time I talked to her before she left for New York.

"Stay."

"Stay with you, Jackson?"

Yes, but I would never say it out loud. I couldn't. It was good she'd left. I took a breath.

"I saw how I'd messed things up and stopped blaming her. It's done."

"Don't you think you should talk to her about this?"

"I've moved on, Dad."

He joined me by the window, putting his hand on my shoulder before he spoke.

"I admire you, Jackson. I admired how you reacted when Kate left. You couldn't make her stay, but you stayed until she was out the door. Most men would have made excuses, but you were honest about your part in it. You accepted your last church's decision to let you go. You took the time to heal, and the change I saw in you was the reason I asked you to come back. Maybe some people had some questions when you first came back, but I don't think they do now. I never did."

"Then you understand why I can't repeat this again?"

"Repeat what? Do you mean that by acknowledging she's back, you'll pick up where you two left off? If that's the case, then you're not making room for redemption. Neither of you are bound to a repeat."

"But that's not how it feels. When I saw Louisa on Sunday, it's like she never left." I shook my head and laughed, not a nice one. "And it's not like I've been sitting around, waiting. After I dealt with what happened, I stopped thinking about it. I haven't been thinking about her, until she showed up. You see something new there, and I'm sorry, but I can't see what you see."

Dad didn't let me finish, his voice kind but firm. "You're wrong about her. She is not the same person who left here a few months ago. You're not the same man, and maybe it's because you've been thrown for a loop, but you aren't sounding like a man who's moved on."

I shook my head. "Being with Rebecca is great. I like her. She's nice. Look at Louisa, and she'll either stare you down or look away. Rebecca smiles and talks to people. She asks them how they're doing. She sees outside of herself and helps people. She believes in God,

———

23

and I don't have to fight her on my beliefs every step of the way. It's not a problem for Rebecca that I'm a pastor."

I looked at Dad. He didn't say anything, but something about how he looked back at me made me wonder whether I'd made my case. I left the window ledge and opened the door to go.

CHAPTER 7: LU

"Did you find anything?" Gracie asked.

"You mean other than confirming Pastor Cleary's matchmaking plan was a job offer? Or are you talking about the boxes?"

"I'm still not convinced it's just a job offer," she speculated, leaning across the island in my parents' kitchen to pluck a carrot from the bag on the counter.

"It takes two to tango," I said.

"You and his dad seem to be getting along."

"We aren't the ones you want to tango. Even if Jackson were interested, opening boxes of old junk made me sneeze all day. It's not a good look."

I pointed to my red nose, but Gracie was undeterred.

"Rudolph came out on top in the end."

This cued the singing of my nieces, who were crafting at the kitchen table with the "Jesus is Groovy" stickers I'd found in one of the boxes from the 1970s.

"What are you doing?" Gracie asked as I rummaged around the pantry.

"Making chicken noodle soup."

She gave me a strange look.

"I talked a bit more with Paul, and the first step of this project is seeing what we have. I spent most of today emptying the boxes and categorizing them. If I'm going by quantity, then church cookbooks warrant their own chapter. I think the church has printed a cookbook every three years, and it's the same ladies contributing repeat recipes with Grandma Pat holding the clear majority. Look at the index."

I handed the 1981 cookbook to Gracie as I moved the carrots a safe distance from her grabby fingers. Now if I could find a peeler. And a knife. And a cutting board. And maybe someone else to cook dinner.

"How come you didn't go for Pat's Jell-O mold?"

"I don't trust fruit that has to hide in mold."

"It's not mold like you're thinking, Lu."

"Why risk it?"

"Why not make the chocolate chip banana bread? She always baked a loaf for my birthday."

"Baking is beyond my skill level."

"You don't bake pierogies," Gracie pointed out, flipping to another page. "And look – there aren't too many ingredients."

"Yes, but it involves dough, which seems like a strange kind of magic."

"I hear you. The only dough I've used comes from a Pillsbury can."

That stopped my utensil search.

"I could go for one of their cinnamon rolls right now."

Gracie popped off her stool. "I have some!"

Which is how Chefs Lu & Gracie came to serve Pillsbury orange cinnamon rolls and homemade chicken noodle soup for dinner that night. It was great, except for the soup part. To my family's credit, no one said anything until I did.

"I think I might have overcooked the noodles," I confessed, poking my spoon around the soup's porridge-like consistency for some of those veggies I'd diced in cubes.

Ted flashed me a "You think?"

Dad was kinder. "Grandma Pat always cooked the noodles separately and ladled them in at the end."

"I didn't see that in the recipe," I said.

"She never included all her tricks," Mom said.

I started laughing. I believed it, but I couldn't believe I hadn't anticipated it.

"It's true," Mom continued. "Compare the church cookbook to her recipe card for chicken noodle soup in the kitchen. Each published recipe is missing something important."

"How'd she justify tricking people like that?"

"Job security," Mom said. "These were her catering recipes."

"Wouldn't that turn people off to the recipes?"

"No," Dad smiled. "It would get people to say things like, 'No one can make that chicken noodle soup like Pat can.'"

"Is job security why the soup doesn't taste like anything?" Caroline asked.

"That part of the recipe was 'salt to taste,'" I said. "I assumed we could do that for ourselves."

When everyone reached for the saltshaker at the same time, I suggested hot dogs for dinner instead, which Mom rounded out with boxed macaroni and cheese.

"Wait a minute, kiddo," Dad said as I was about to pour the pot of soup down the drain after dinner.

"You want me to save this?"

"No, I don't want you to pour it down the garbage disposal. The noodles will expand and clog it."

He produced a tower of quart-sized yogurt containers from under the kitchen sink, where Grandma stored her plasticware – a motley assortment of yogurt, sour cream, margarine and other containers she cleaned for reuse. I ran my fingers along the faded logo of one, wondering how many washes it had seen.

Dad smiled, knowing my thoughts. "That was your grandma. She never got over those years of raising me by herself and watching every penny. Guess how much money we found hidden around her rooms when we cleaned them out?"

"You mean …"

I swallowed, trying to clear my head. I pointed to the closed door off the kitchen that led to the suite of rooms Dad built for Grandma when she moved in to help raise Ted and me.

"The rooms are empty?"

He nodded.

It made sense. Of course Dad and Mom wouldn't have kept everything as is after so many months, but the thought felt like a void. I'd been quick to visit Grandma Pat's grave, but her rooms, emptied, was something to work around, like how being with my family without her was something to work around.

I wiped the tears from my eyes and started to line up the yogurt containers. Dad followed behind, pouring out the soup.

"Where did all of her things go?"

"Grandma left a list. You can imagine how your mother felt about taking care of that." Dad raised his eyebrows.

"Were people happy to have it?" I could see how they would be, but most of Grandma's possessions were used when they came to her. She'd made them special by arrangement. In ones and twos, it was more like a white elephant gift exchange.

"You remember how filled the church was at her funeral? Grandma Pat helped a lot of people, and they couldn't believe she'd think to give them something. Even Nana, though she'd never admit it."

"What did she leave Nana?"

They came from worlds as different as a small town could hold. Grandma was the daughter of poor Polish immigrants who'd never learned to speak English. She'd made a living on her sewing and cooking skills. Nana was the country club. Or at least the mansion she lived in across town was about as big as the country club.

"She left her an old, painted turquoise dresser. I have no idea why, and I expected Nana to tell me to haul it to the dump, but she told me to leave it in her foyer. I think it's still there."

I knew the piece – it was the dresser from Grandma's bedroom, and it didn't go with anything in Nana's house, but right now I was still taken by the thought of Grandma's empty rooms.

"You want to move down from the attic?" Dad asked, misinterpreting the looks I kept flicking at Grandma's closed door.

"No. I'm surprised she didn't tell you who to leave those rooms to, though."

"I think that might have been wishful thinking on her part."

"What do you mean?"

"Grandma Pat also left you something, Lu."

"What?" With her, it could be anything. There was no point in guessing.

"Her shop, Penny Thrift."

CHAPTER 8: LU

I worshipped Grandma Pat when I was a little girl. She had a golden touch, minus the gold. It was more that she could cook basics into something wonderful. I never minded taking pungent leftovers of stuffed cabbage for school lunch. When my friends unrolled their My Little Pony or Barbie sleeping bags for sleepovers, I'd unfold a quilt she'd pieced from yard-sale fabrics. It was beautiful – we all thought so – and special because it was unique, like everything she sewed.

When Grandma moved into our home, Dad converted her ranch into her store: Penny Thrift. She'd made her living as a seamstress for years, but it wasn't until she opened the shop that people saw her design skills. She had a knack for forming new work from old – pieces from this curtain and that sheet – to make quilts, throw pillows, tablecloths, or another curtain. Grandma didn't create to mimic what everyone else was selling, and I don't think selling her creations was the primary goal, either. Every item was a chance to see whether she could make something out of nothing.

She thrifted all of her fabrics, and her creations cost her nothing but time. Even at the end of a day – after she ran her shop, helped us with homework, and cooked dinner – she'd sit down with sewing. I loved to watch her stitch. She was fast and precise. I couldn't understand the hours she put into repetition, but it paid off. When I'd returned from New York last summer, Penny Thrift was selling nationwide.

By the time she was my age, Grandma Pat was raising my dad in a house she'd bought herself with the profit from the sewing and catering businesses she'd started. I grimaced to think of where I was in comparison.

I badgered Dad with questions throughout the week, starting with why hadn't they told me? Why hadn't she told me? This seemed like the sort of inheritance you might want to run by the recipient: technically, co-recipient. That was also news. Ted and I were co-owners. The family had decided not to tell me any of this or do anything about Penny Thrift other than fulfilling outstanding orders and closing down the web site after I left for New York.

"We thought you had enough to deal with," Ted said. "It seemed like you were trying to figure out whether to stay in New York, and we didn't want to confuse that decision with something that could bring you back here if you didn't want to be here otherwise. It's not like we needed to figure out anything immediately. The shop is paid off. It's not going anywhere."

Still, a part of me would prefer the turquoise dresser Grandma left Nana. It was a simpler gift and would make a great replacement for the three-drawer white one that held only half of my clothes. Come Friday, I decided to use Mom as my mediator in this barter. She handed me the keys to the store before I finished my first sentence.

"Before you decide to exchange a business for a dresser, go take a look. Pick up some pizza at Creek's on your way home. We also need a gallon of milk."

I did as told, if for no reason other than to avoid spending Friday night with my parents. Light from the street followed me in through the front door, but even in the dimness, I could see nothing had changed.

I stood in the entryway for a long time, looking around. The shelves to the left always featured the newest fabric finds – an inventory that would change weekly. It was strange to think these fabrics, which Grandma had pressed, folded, and paired in tidy rows, had been here for months. To the right stood a large wooden table, with a thick butcher block top and square legs, for cutting and piecing. To the back was the register and behind that the small kitchen Dad kept intact so Grandma could multi-task between her sewing and catering businesses. Last were the basement stairs she'd fallen down that resulted in me standing here as owner instead of her.

I kept to the front. The store was inspiring, but all the pretty fabrics in the world weren't going to change the fact that I didn't know how to design or sew. I couldn't finish the quilt Grandma had started piecing on the table. If someone were to ask me to cut a yard of fabric, I'd have to think about the math.

Of course the maddening part of it all was my family, who seemed to have opinions about everything, but were open when it came to the shop. Ted wanted me to think about it for awhile. When I pressed Dad this week, he'd reminded me it wasn't his decision to make.

I wandered the shelves, unfolding and re-folding fabric, but other than noting its potential in someone else's hands, I had no ideas. The hour I spent in these stacks wasn't that different from my work at church all week. Nothing had taken shape there, either, other than moving everything from boxes to piles. There was the cookbook pile, the annual report pile, and the annual meeting minute pile, which sat next to the elders' meeting pile. I lumped the minutes from all other church committees in a corner of the room. There was also the photo directory pile, which I'd lingered over for a couple hours. I flipped to Jackson's family's photos after laughing over mine. I remembered how he'd always worn shirts buttoned straight to the neck, but I'd forgotten his glasses.

By the time I returned home, I was no farther along in figuring out what to do with it all. Making decisions about Penny Thrift felt like one project too many, but that's not a reason to unload a store or exchange it for a dresser.

My phone buzzed with Mom's reminder. Time to get to the rest of my Friday night – pizza, milk, and my parents.

"As I live and breathe, if it isn't Lu Sokolowski," a voice shouted from across Creek's Pizzeria after I'd ordered a double pepperoni to go. A whistle followed, and I turned to see Jackson. The shout and whistle came from the man beside him – Rodney Asher Morton III. Or was it IV? It's an impossible name, regardless, which is why he went by Roddy.

Not that I'd ever used either. I only knew *of* Roddy because I'm a girl, and every girl in Dunlap's Creek – and maybe, the world – knows of Roddy.

He had dark brown, almost black, hair with a touch of wave and ice blue eyes, now bordered with wrinkles that made him more appealing than when I'd last seen him in high school. He was the kind of handsome that makes you want to know what he looked like with his shirt off. Something in his eyes dared it, and a larger part told you he'd oblige. I knew that much about him.

We had a loose connection. Roddy was the only child of parents who ran the largest construction company in the area. They contracted people like my dad for work.

I didn't know about the Jackson connection. Jackson and I hadn't run with the same people growing up, and since we'd both returned to Dunlap's Creek around the same time last summer, neither of us had a crowd. Still, I assumed his people would be more churchy and less Roddy.

I walked over, and Roddy pulled out a chair.

"Join us?"

I looked at Jackson. We'd seen each other a couple times at church this week, but he was either with someone else or the construction noise negated conversation. Of course, the real reason we didn't talk was I'd left my big-girl pants at home all week. Whatever courage I'd had after Nana pushed me forward last Sunday was gone, and Jackson's polite smiles told me I'd reached the statute of limitations for clearing the air.

He gave me another one now, and I sat, trying not to think about how the next few minutes could go. I ran with the question of the moment.

"You two know each other?"

Roddy pulled his chair close and leaned in, replacing one anxiety with another. He smelled as good he looked. Then he smiled. I'd forgotten the dimples. Now my cheeks were red.

Roddy smiled wider. "You aren't the first person to ask that question. It goes back to scouts. Jackson's dad enrolled him to learn about personal responsibility."

"And Roddy's father enrolled him because …" Jackson prompted.

"Because he didn't know what the hell else to do with me. It was a good thing, too, because when the preacher's kid couldn't pitch a tent, guess who saved him? In return, Jackson's been trying to save my soul ever since. He takes the parable of the lost sheep a little too seriously."

"You know that parable?"

"I played football for St. Ignatius, remember?"

I shook my head. "I haven't kept tabs."

Roddy put his hand to his chest in mock hurt, drawing my eyes there. I could look at this man all day. He smiled; he knew it.

"I would have kept tabs on you, Lu, but your brother would have killed me. Didn't he marry that cute little cheerleader? What was her name?"

"Gracie. I'll make sure to send him your regards."

"I'm not scared of Ted anymore."

"I came home last summer," I pointed out. "You never hit on me then."

"I was managing a project across the state. By the time I came back, I believe a claim was staked."

I followed Roddy's eyes to Jackson, whose face gave away nothing. The noise of the restaurant made our silence louder. Roddy cut it by turning his dimpled smile back at me.

"Or at least that's what I thought."

The counter called his name, and he left to get their pizza. I looked at Jackson. Roddy's opening was as good as any I'd had all week, and I pushed myself to take it.

"Jackson, I want to ..."

"How's the anniversary book coming along?" he asked, leaning back in his chair and cutting me off.

I didn't want to talk about the book, especially since it wasn't coming along so much as piling up. Jackson didn't bother to wait for my answer to his inane question before he pulled out his phone to text someone, probably Rebecca. By the time he looked up, Roddy was back, and Creek's was calling my name.

"Leaving so soon?" Roddy asked as I stood. He stepped close and the forced smile I'd planted on my face to say goodbye turned into a real one. I wasn't interested in Roddy, but my few minutes here were the most fun I'd had all week.

"You want my number?" he asked.

The question dispelled the tension. I laughed and shook my head. Before leaving, I pointed from Roddy to Jackson.

"You two make no sense."

I took my pizza to go.

CHAPTER 9: JACKSON

"You're an ass," Roddy said right before he grabbed the largest slice off the platter. "Don't deny it."

"I didn't say anything."

"That's the point. You open your life to everyone, but you won't talk about her."

"Ask whatever you want."

"I don't need to. Lu's face said everything. I would know. I've pissed off a lot of women."

Louisa was going to say something I wasn't sure I wanted to hear, so I changed the subject. When my phone buzzed, I pulled it out like a reflex, but it came across as rude. I needed to apologize.

"She's gorgeous," Roddy continued. "You see that, right? Your little church brain isn't denying that?"

I returned his stare. "You have a knack for talking like you're asking for a punch in the face."

"Which is why my only friend believes in turning the other cheek."

"Taken out of context, as usual. Why are we talking about this? I've never asked about your …" I was about to say relationships, but Roddy didn't have those.

He wiped his hands on a napkin and smiled at me. "I'd be happy to confess."

"Spilling the details isn't the same thing, and I'm not your priest, Roddy. I'm your friend.

Roddy sat back and folded his arms across his chest. "Exactly."

There it was. Roddy was my friend; the kind of friend you wanted to punch in the face because he told the truth, and he had from day one. I was the preacher's kid in a small town. Most people treated me like it, but Roddy took it as a dare. What he got us into as kids was tame, at least compared to what he did when he grew up. Roddy played hard, and we'd lost touch for most of high school and college, but that didn't stop him from telling me I was making a mistake when I asked Kate to marry me. I ignored him. He came to my wedding anyway, and then again to my house after my divorce, boxing up what was left and never saying a word about it. We've hung out ever since.

"What do you want to know, Roddy?"

"I know it all."

"Then what do you want to say?"

"I already said it. Plus, don't we have to eat this pizza and go to your girlfriend's? Isn't she making us brownies?"

I shook my head as I bit into my first piece. "I'm not responding to that."

"Didn't think you would. Can I have Lu's number?"

I recited it without a thought.

"Isn't this the part where you call her first to warn her about me?" he asked.

"I've found that has the opposite effect."

"What about the part where you tell me to keep my hands off?"

"Trust me. Louisa Sokolowski can take care of herself."

CHAPTER 10: LU

I'm not sure why I sought Nana for a second opinion. I rarely appreciated her unsolicited ones. But Saturday morning, I drove to her house across town and asked her to come with me to Penny Thrift. I did my best to ignore the turquoise dresser standing between us in the foyer.

"I am busy today, Louisa."

Cue mental eye roll. "Doing what?"

"This and that."

"For example?"

"Never you mind."

She shooed me away with her manicured hand, but I leaned my arms on the top of the dresser and tapped it with my unpolished fingers.

"Can I have this?'

"Why ever would you want an old dresser?"

I widened my eyes. "You mean this old dresser? The one in the middle of your foyer?" I was not exaggerating. It stood like a shabby-chic target in the center of Nana's marbled and pillared foyer – a case study of spare splendor. Even my nieces would know which of these items didn't belong.

I persisted. "I wish she'd left me the dresser."

"She left you the store. That's plenty."

"The store no one told me about."

"We thought you had enough going on."

"I don't want the store."

"You need the store. You don't need this dresser."

"You do?"

This place had six bedrooms, all with dressers. Nana nodded anyway.

I stopped tapping my fingers and looked at her. The differences between my grandmas went beyond their backgrounds. Grandma Pat always spoke her mind. Nana locked up her thoughts. She'd let the nod out, but she wasn't going to say anything else. I retreated from the dresser, opened the front door, and gestured outside.

"Care to convince me a closed shop is more useful than a dresser?"

She straightened the muted pink jacket of her Saturday morning suit. "On two conditions. First, we take my car."

"What's wrong with the car you bought me?" Nana, like the rest of my family, hadn't been in favor of my returning to New York with John, but she'd replaced my '85 Cutlass with a new Civic so I could get there in one piece.

"I prefer mine. And second, you'll owe me a favor in return."

At this point, I questioned whether she was doing me a favor. I herded her to the Caddy before she could change her mind.

Nana took a seat next to the project table, crossing her ankles and folding her hands on her lap. I kept to the door, watching her eyes wander Penny Thrift, wondering what she saw.

"I've never worked a job in my life," she concluded after several minutes of silence.

I believed it. Grandpa had died when I was 13, and Nana moved into our house the day after the burial without an explanation. It wasn't until Grandma Pat died last winter that she moved back to her house. Fifteen years she'd lived with us, and I'd never seen her do a scrap of work other than make her bed.

"In my day, women in my position didn't work outside the home."

I'd heard this preamble before, and I waited for the part where she told me to find a rich man to marry. What worked for her should work for me – that was her party line.

Nana surprised me.

"That's not how it is anymore, Lu. If you're going to stay here, you need to work. This shop gives you work."

With that, she walked out the front door. The woman had an uncanny ability to conclude a conversation I thought we were just starting. I scrambled to turn off the lights and lock the door.

"How am I going to do it?" I asked as we settled in the car and fastened our seatbelts.

"I have no idea."

We didn't say anything else on the drive back to her place. The silence continued as I parked the car in the detached garage, opened her door, and followed her along the brick pathway to the double wooden doors of her house.

Nana turned to me before going inside. "Please pick me up at five."

"For what?"

"L'Etoile Printemps at the Country Club."

"I understood half that sentence."

"The annual spring social."

"I never agreed to that."

"You owe me a favor," she reminded me.

"You never told me what it was."

"You never asked. You should learn to clarify negotiations before you go into business. Make sure you don't wear any of your usual outfits. They don't suit."

And she shut the door.

I had descended into wearing sloppy casual in Dunlap's Creek, so I could see Nana's point about my clothes, but her daily uniform of designer two-pieces made me insecure about my far nattier New York wardrobe.

"She won't like that," Mom said when I came downstairs in black cigarette pants and a white, sleeveless blouse.

"It's silk." And pristine, though I'd scored it for $10 at a vintage resale in New York. I loved the top almost as much as the bargain.

"It's white before Memorial Day, and with the black pants, Nana will think you match the waiters at the Club. Also, she doesn't like it when women wear pants. You know this."

"It's the 21st century."

"Not to her."

"And they're slacks."

"They might as well be dungarees."

"Well, aren't you stubborn."

"Not me," Mom said. "Trust me, I grew up with her. I can't believe you're going to this thing."

"I think she wants company. She must be lonely living by herself. Do you want to go instead?"

Her look was a no, so back upstairs I went to thumb through my clothes for the 27th time. Fifteen minutes later I settled on my most recent clothing purchase – a black dress I'd bought for John's firm party on what ended up as my last night in New York. It was my LBD answer to whatever Chanel suit Nana would wear and by far the nicest item in my wardrobe. It came with memories, though – memories that Nana unwittingly referenced when I arrived at her door.

"Isn't that a little provocative, Lu? Let me get you a jacket."

I shook my head and ushered her into the car, though I felt a touch of relief when I saw what other girls my age were wearing when we arrived at the club. At least my midriff wasn't showing I almost commented, but the sheer splendor of the dining room stopped any conversation – legitimate china and crystal, silver candelabras, and packed vases of peonies I wanted to bury my nose in like a dog. Nana and Grandpa paraded me around the Club when I was little and willing to wear sailor dresses with matching berets. She took a break after he died. By the time she re-entered, I was in a Goth period and painting my nails black, so she brought Grandma Pat instead.

Grandma would have stuck out here as much as her dresser did in Nana's foyer. She never wore pastel – the color of choice for tonight's gathering – because it didn't go with her flaming red hair. She never wore something she didn't make, and she pieced her clothes like quilts.

"What are you smiling about?" Nana asked as I pulled out her chair.

"Grandma Pat in this place. How did that work?"

Nana didn't answer but adjusted her silverware by small increments. She took a sip from her crystal goblet of ice water, then turned to me, her face devoid of expression but for a glint in her eyes.

"She handled it like no one else."

She looked away and said in as close to a mutter as I've ever heard from her, "Pat never cared what other people thought about her, including this crowd."

I wanted to ask more, but the rest of our table arrived: three generations of handsome, ending with none other than Roddy himself. He hung back as Nana made the introductions in order of age, and by the time he extended his hand in greeting, his eyes and smile relayed nothing other than polite interest. The sole woman in their party, Roddy's mother, Barbara, was the first to open conversation.

"It's nice to see you again, Lu. What brings you back to Dunlap's Creek?"

That was as good a conversation stumper as any for me. Nana stepped in.

"Pat left Penny Thrift to Lu and her brother, Ted."

Barbara nodded.

"The shop with the secondhand goods?"

I opened my mouth to object, but Nana beat me to it.

"Pat sold her designs nationwide."

She'd kept her tone neutral, but the immediacy of her response made me wonder how often she'd defended Grandma here. Her gaze leveled like a staring contest poor Barbara wasn't ready to play. Barbara finished as politely as possible.

"Pat was an important part of this town. I'm sorry about your loss, Lu."

"Me, too."

Those two words were my first and last contribution to the dinner conversation. Normally, I'd wish for a book stowed in my purse for moments like these, but Nana's excuse for my return kept my mind busy with a question. Could I run Penny Thrift? If I had the guts to ask it out loud, the men at this table would answer me. Roddy's grandfather had started the business they were still expanding. They would know the answer to my question, but I was afraid they'd say it in business lingo I wouldn't understand, or worse, ask about my non-existent qualifications.

Dinner ended and the orchestral set stepped up their volume. Dancing time, which was the perfect time to excuse myself for the bathroom. I turned to go and found myself face-to-face with Roddy.

"Would you like to dance?" he asked.

I shook my head before inclining it toward Nana, my scapegoat.

He directed his question to her. "Mrs. Williams, do you mind if I steal your granddaughter for a dance?"

Her smile said she'd let him steal me to Mexico.

He led me to the dance floor, but I held up my finger once we stepped onto it. He smiled, with his dimples in full splendor. Pizza Parlor Roddy was back.

"Before we dance, I have some ground rules. First, this is just a dance."

"If you say so."

"It is not leaving this floor."

"Unless you change your mind."

"Which isn't going to happen."

"Because you want to be with someone who's with someone else?" he asked.

"That's the next rule. I'm not talking about Jackson."

"I find it interesting neither of you are talking. Jack is an open book, except when it comes to you, and I can already tell I won't get anywhere with you."

"Why's that?"

"You're still giving me the rules."

Roddy extended his hand, and I realized I was still holding up my finger like a school marm. I retracted it and stepped into his arms, hoping he could dance well enough for both of us since most of the women here were waiting for me to fall on my face.

"You didn't need Ted to protect you growing up. You're scary enough to keep any man away."

I laughed. "That's what Jackson said."

"Interesting. Want to talk more about it? What Jack said and under what conditions?"

"No."

He shook his head. "You church people."

He stopped talking and his eyes scanned the room. Of course Roddy would lump me into that crowd, given my family and Jackson. A week ago, I would have been quick to correct him. I tapped his shoulder.

"Finish your thought."

He brought his blue eyes back to mine.

"You make the simple complicated," he said.

"How so?"

"You don't let a dance be a dance. And you definitely don't let anything happen after the dance."

"That's an excuse for you to do whatever you want with whomever you want, Roddy. There's another half to your story that makes it less simple."

"Care to ask any of the women around here?"

"I don't want to know how many women could give me an answer. And no," I said, lifting my finger back up as he opened his mouth. "I don't want names. It's bad enough they're staring daggers into my back."

He looked around again, and after a few seconds, his eyes returned to mine. "They are looking at you."

"More like through me to get back to you," I noted. "See, it's not as simple as you claim."

"Or I'm that good. Care to try?"

I shook my head. "Didn't you mention something last night about a hands-off policy when a claim's been staked?"

He met my joke without hesitation.

"That was last summer and before I went to Jack's girlfriend's house and ate her homemade brownies."

He won, and I looked down. I'd rather Roddy go back to name-calling than hear more about Jack's girlfriend's house. The chocolate sounded good, though. I wondered whether Rebecca put frosting on her brownies.

"There you go again," he said.

"What?"

"Making it complicated. You can look down and pretend you don't care about what I said. Or you could simplify all of this with one visit to Jack's place in that dress you're wearing."

"That wouldn't work."

"He's a man, Lu."

I looked back at Roddy. He returned it without apology or pretense.

"I do make things complicated," I admitted. And then I shook my head and laughed. "I make things ridiculously complicated, but that doesn't have anything to do with being a 'church person,' as you put it. I'm sure if you came to church tomorrow instead of leaving with one of these girls tonight, you'd see all kinds of people – simple and complicated."

He winked at me. "I can do both."

The song ended, and I stepped away from Roddy to walk the social rounds with Nana. It was another hour of small talk, and I noticed he was gone before we left. I didn't know with which girl; the sidelines had been pretty packed.

I'd tossed out the church offer as a joke. I assumed Roddy had responded in kind, so I was surprised to see him waiting at the end of my driveway the next morning, leaning against his car — shiny, red, and so low to the ground I questioned whether it was decent for me to attempt entry in my skirt.

"I told you I could do both."

"You don't expect me to go to church in this car?"

"Should I have brought the Beemer instead?"

"I prefer to fly under the radar."

"And how's that working for you?" He opened the passenger door.

I ignored the question. "We need to pick up Nana on the way."

CHAPTER 11: JACKSON

"What causes someone to lie?" I asked to open Sunday's sermon. "We're in the second half of Genesis 12, if you'd like to open your Bibles and read along. If you don't have one, feel free to grab one in the pew pocket in front of you."

"Let's recap. Abram had work, a life, and family in Ur, a prosperous ancient city, but he gave it up when God called him to go. It was a bold move, one that causes us to ask whether we're willing to do the same. But fast-forward a few verses, and Abram is off to Egypt – a place God never told him to go – with his wife, Sarah, whom he's now calling his "sister.""

"Following God is never simple, but Abram made it impossible by going his own way. Why the detour?"

One of the first things I learned about preaching in seminary was it put pastors on the front lines. God doesn't want hypocrites in the pulpit. Louisa's return pushed me to having the conversation with Rebecca I'd been putting off for so long it felt like a lie. I had it as soon as the church emptied last Sunday.

"Can we talk?"

Rebecca sat next to me on the pew, waiting for me to begin. I looked down at my hands, unsure of how to sum up Louisa and me.

"That woman you met – Louisa – she's from here, but came home from New York last summer. She ended up going back to New York this past winter after her grandma died, but before that, we spent a lot of time together ... we spent most of our time together, and ..."

This explanation was going from bad to worse, and I looked up to see how it was playing out with Rebecca. She smiled, and it cut my tension.

"Are you going to help me out here?" I asked.

"I was wondering if you were ever going to look up from your lap."

"I haven't been honest with you."

She put her hand on mine. "I haven't told you about everyone I've been with."

It was an easy out, but I shook my head. "This is different than what you're talking about."

Her smile left. "How so?"

"Because Louisa was important to me, and I wanted – hoped – things would be different between us, but all of this," I said looking around the church, "wasn't for her."

Rebecca took her hand away but kept her eyes on mine. "I saw how she looked at you, Jackson. What if she's back because she changed her mind?"

"She left to be with her ex-boyfriend," I answered, but Rebecca let out a small laugh.

"That doesn't settle anything."

I smiled. "Maybe not for Louisa, but that's too complicated for me."

"And I'm simple?"

She knew what I meant, and she'd asked the question lightly – not to catch me, Rebecca wasn't like that – to move us along. It's hard to mess up with a woman who says what she thinks as plainly as she can, and I hadn't known what that could be like until her. With my ex-wife, words were clues I never pieced correctly, and with Louisa, words were sharp, a challenge. Rebecca held out hers out like offerings and her life like an invitation. I'd wanted to step into it since the first day I met her.

I traced her cheek with my finger. Even now, with her uncertainty, there was warmth. Light. This quality more than any other separated her from Louisa. Rebecca wanted to believe me.

"You're as whole a person as I've ever met, and I want to be with you," I said. "What happened with Louisa happened. I know enough now to stay away."

I'd held my end this past week and kept my distance – despite my dad, despite Roddy. I thought a lot about today's sermon passage from Genesis. It was easy to judge Abram for going to Egypt, but I saw him differently than I had before, less willful. I think he wanted to walk the path God had laid out, but he got scared.

In Abram's case, it was fear of famine; for me, it was a girl. I assumed Louisa would be at church this morning because she was working for the church. Her family sat on the left, and so far, I'd kept my eyes to the right where Rebecca sat. We hadn't talked about Louisa again, and as far as I could tell, everything between us was normal.

But it's not normal if I'm refusing to look at half the church.

"Fear can change the course. God told Abram he will make him into a great nation. But there's famine – severe famine – in this land where he's told him to go. God's call seems at cross-purposes with basic survival. How can Abram become a great nation without food?"

I looked left and saw Louisa's parents and her nana.

"It makes sense he'd go where the food is. No one would criticize him for this decision, except there are two problems. One, Egypt is not where God told him to go. Two, Abram has to lie to get in. His wife is too pretty. They'll kill him to get to her."

I saw Ted and Gracie.

"He can't solve the first problem, but he makes a plan to solve the second: *Say you are my sister,* he tells his wife, *so that I will be treated well for your sake and my life will be spared because of you.* There's a lot of "my" and "I" in his plan, isn't there? It's tempting to judge him because on one hand, Abram is God's chosen patriarch. He's a big deal, and a big deal shouldn't be so concerned with his stomach. But his plan shows us he's still a man."

I saw Louisa and paused at the sight of her for the second Sunday in a row – at a better point in the sermon. But the reason I paused wasn't because of her this time. What was Roddy doing here?

He found me right after service. Lu was behind him, I doubt by choice.

"Lu and I were out together last night …"

She stepped forward to clarify.

"We happened to be at the same place," she said.

"She asked me to take her to church."

"As a joke, and I said 'go' to church, not 'take' me here."

"And here I am, no joke." Roddy smiled, putting his arm around her. "But we have to run because she invited me over for lunch."

"I did not."

She shrugged his arm off and stepped to the side. He looked at her, his face the perfect picture of rejection.

"I'm not invited?"

"You can come, but …"

"Great. Nice preaching, Jack. And there's the lovely Rebecca. I didn't see you, darling. What do you and Jackson have planned for today?"

Roddy took Rebecca aside to answer that question, leaving Louisa and me alone with each other, except for everyone else who hadn't left church yet. That was the major flaw in Roddy's plan, but he'd railroaded us all the same. We smiled at the same time, like friends do, and I was about to ask about her plans for the day when my phone buzzed in my back pocket, reminding me.

"I'm sorry about the phone the other night."

The ease left with her smile.

"You're apologizing to me about the phone?" she asked, but it sounded more like a challenge.

"I also cut you off when you started to tell me something. What did you want to tell me?"

It was a question I needed to ask, but not here. It cut the conversation around us, and now, Roddy, Rebecca, and a handful of others were waiting for her to respond. Louisa wasn't going to. I knew that before she turned away.

How many times could I mess up with one woman? Roddy knew enough not to call me out in the middle of church, but his look said it before he stepped in.

"To be continued, then. Lunch, Lu?"

She didn't look at me again before they left.

CHAPTER 12: LU

"You promised me simple, Lu," Roddy said, leaning against the counter and watching me unload vegetables from the fridge for Chicken Noodle Soup 2.0.

He'd invited himself to lunch, but it felt insufficient to serve cold cuts on his first meal here, especially after he rescued me when it went quiet after church. Granted, none of that would have happened if he'd followed me out of church instead of pulling me forward.

"This soup doesn't have that many ingredients."

"I was talking about the sermon, not the soup."

"And what was so complicated about the sermon?"

"The whole wife-sister angle? Even I've never done that."

Gracie's family arrived from next door, cutting my need to respond and occupying the ladies' man with enough girls to charm for the next hour while I cross-referenced Grandma's recipe from three cookbooks. Only one mentioned cooking the noodles separately, and all three used different salt measurements. I opted for the "salt to taste" instruction again, but on the front-end, and I would have continued with adding one salt crystal at a time if not for Ted.

"If you don't move this along, I'm going to smash Roddy's face in. It's bad enough you brought him to church."

"He brought me," I whispered, hoping Ted would lower his volume so our guest, who was engaging in a Who's Who of Dunlap's Creek with Nana, wouldn't hear. Not that Roddy would care, at least not like how I cared about the heaping spoon of salt Ted was pouring into the stockpot.

"Ted!" I shrieked, putting my hands to my cheeks. "What have you done?"

"Made your soup taste like something."

He dipped the same spoon into the soup and held it to my mouth for a sample. I expected the broth equivalent of a Sour Patch Kid, but Ted was right. It tasted like legitimate soup. I noted "soup spoon with a half-inch dome" in the church cookbook I'd designated for master recipes and called lunch.

It took a special person to fit into a Sokolowski family meal. Today's began before it started with my youngest niece draining her first glass of milk and requesting another before our butts hit the seats. While Ted tended to that, my middle niece, Abigail, asked for ketchup. I was about to question the pairing, but Gracie's headshake told me to keep quiet. Then the pregnant lady remembered she had to pee one more time before we ate. While she was away, Mom blamed me for not setting napkins on the table, though she was the one who set it.

"As a favor to you, Lu." It was my Sunday chore, and I was still 12-years-old, apparently.

Roddy smiled through it all and offered to get Holly her third glass of milk when it was the last task between our meal and us. Dad said grace, and our corporate hunger bought us one spoonful of blessed silence before Caroline asked the question.

"Are you Aunt Lu's new boyfriend?"

She'd insisted on sitting next to him and put her hand on his when she asked the question. Ted glared. I smiled.

"Not yet," Roddy responded.

"He doesn't mean that," I explained for the benefit of the table.

"Good!" Caroline exclaimed. There was still hope for her.

Ted made her switch seats, despite Gracie's warning look about table manners. This was why Dad, in a rare maneuver, took over the conversation with construction talk. Normally debates of pressure treated versus untreated lumber made for a snooze fest, but the deeper they talked shop, the more natural the conversation felt. Even Ted stopped acting like a bear.

The real surprise for me was Roddy. Roddy was smart and driven, and his role in the family business wasn't nepotism. He'd earned his way in, first through working construction sites at the same pay rate as everyone else. The projects he talked about at lunch were bids he'd won — the majority of which were out of town and many of those, out of state.

Dad and Ted were craftsman first and businessmen a distant second. Roddy was all business. He hadn't worked construction longer than necessary, and he didn't need to because he was more interested in running a business to make a living than building something with his hands. Their conversation sparked a new thought. I didn't have to know how to sew to run Penny Thrift well, and I now I knew who to ask.

"My place?" Roddy asked after I walked him to his car after lunch.

I sat on the hood without thinking about it.

"Don't sit there," he said, his tone clipped.

"Can you help me with something?"

"As long as you get off my car. Right now."

"You do realize you give the impression you'd like this girl-on-the-hood-of-your-car scenario?"

"Not with this car, and I doubt your sitting on it is going to turn out how I'm thinking."

"Gross."

"Don't start games you can't finish."

He smiled but crooked his finger. I complied after a pat to the hood.

"What did you want to ask me?"

"My grandma's shop — the one with the 'second-hand goods?' She left it to Ted and me, and we're trying to figure out what to do with it. Well, me mostly. Ted doesn't care."

"You want to run it?"

"I want to think about it."

"I'd do it."

"You have an MBA. I don't."

"Did your grandma?"

"No, but she knew the craft. Plus, she'd worked in the industry for years. She knew what to charge for her time and for her designs. She had customers on opening day. I don't have any of that."

"All you need to do is figure out how to make money," he said. He started talking about units of sale, price of units, and about ten other things I didn't understand. My mind wandered.

"Are you listening?"

I shook my head. "Not until you say something helpful."

"What do you think I've been talking about for the last five minutes?"

"I have no clue."

He looked at me – a real one, I think his first. It made me more nervous.

"You're a smart girl, Lu," he said after a minute. "Look through your grandma's records and do the math. You'll start to figure this out. If you have any questions, call me."

He leaned down to kiss my cheek before moving me out of his way to get in the car.

"And Lu?" he called as I walked up the driveway. I turned and smiled, feeling like I had a friend.

"Your soup was almost as good as Rebecca's brownies."

"Lu, not that guy," Ted said the second I stepped back into the kitchen. He was playing Uno at the table with the girls while Gracie finished washing the stockpot. I helped her dry.

"Obviously, Ted. He's fun, though. I could use some fun."

"I agree with Lu," Gracie pitched in.

"Which part?"

"He's fun, and she could use some fun."

"Not like that. Not with him. Don't think I didn't notice how he was looking at you." He pointed to Gracie with this last statement.

"At least it distracted him from noticing how I was looking at Roddy," she whispered to me.

I burst out laughing at the same time Ted asked, "What's that?"

"Step down, Ted. I'm seven months pregnant. I'm pretty sure he wasn't looking at me like how you think … at least not in the way he was looking at your sister."

Gracie and I were both laughing when Nana Bea entered the room.

"What a nice young man. Don't you all agree?"

CHAPTER 13: LU

The quilt Grandma Pat pieced from her mom's clothes was the one people always wanted, but she'd never sell. It was a mix of patterns and colors cut into small hexagons and reconstructed in concentric circles to form flower after flower. The quilt totaled thirty-two flowers, and Grandma bound them all with a bright orange fabric that should have come with a disclaimer to use sparingly.

It worked. Grandma knew how to piece it like she knew where to place it – behind the register at Penny Thrift where women could muse over their favorite flower while they waited, like I was doing now.

Over the years, Grandma hired local women to work at Penny Thrift, and if they had talent, she'd sell their items on consignment at a 50/50 split. I discovered all of this when I reviewed her books this past week. Mom and Dad were out of town, and instead of going home to an empty house, I came here. Roddy was right, Grandma's tidy spreadsheets explained the numbers behind her business. There was no mortgage, and the thrifted fabric costs were negligible. The only real expense was labor, which Grandma had done by herself in the beginning, but outsourced more as she got older. In the last several years, she offset this cost by growing her sales online.

Even with hiring out all the sewing and halving the profit with Ted, we'd make money. It wasn't enough to sustain either of us, but it was enough to try, assuming we could produce something people wanted to buy as much as they'd wanted Grandma's designs.

I called Virginia Stanley and asked her to come to the shop tonight to talk about working for me. I'd met her when I returned to Dunlap's Creek last summer. Actually, I met her work first – a beautiful skirt she'd deconstructed from used indigo and white t-shirts and sewn back together in a mess of embroidery and appliqué. Like Grandma's quilt behind the register, the skirt shouldn't have worked, but it did, and I'd worn it to every wedding I'd covered for the paper last year. I was wearing it today, and if I owned any of her other clothes, I'd have piled those on to sway her to work in the shop.

She knocked on the front door, and I opened it to see her, her toddler son, Danny, and a package. Virginia carried her recycling chic to the wrapping, too. Her skirt had come to me in a brown grocery bag decorated in spray painted graffiti. She used newspaper this time.

I peeled apart the tape and caught my breath as soon as I saw what was inside – giant orange roosters reverse appliquéd under white cotton. I'd commissioned these napkins from her as a gift for Grandma last Thanksgiving.

I held the top napkin to my nose and breathed – breathing in that day when my family was whole and Jackson met me at the front door of my house with a single flower. On that day I could talk to him, unlike now with so many layers of unspoken words choking the simplest conversation.

The napkins brought the distance between then and now into sharp relief. Breathing turned to crying, and Virginia hugged me without hesitation. She'd been one of the many people to speak at Grandma's funeral, sharing how Grandma had helped her get back on her feet after Danny's father left. I sent her a thank you note along with these napkins before I returned to New York.

For safekeeping, I'd explained.

She probably assumed I was crying about all of that, and I was – plus everything else. It was a dramatic start for a job interview.

"So, you want to work for me?" I asked, wiping tears from my eyes a few minutes later.

She smiled and didn't say anything but looked at the quilt behind the register. There were two sides to Virginia, which I'd discovered when I profiled her for a story in the paper last summer. Dig too deep with questions, and she'd go quiet, but put fabric in front of her, and she was decisive and bold. The second was the Virginia I needed to help me run the shop.

I turned to the quilt behind the register.

"Which is your favorite flower?"

She pointed without hesitation to a flower pieced with geometric, striped, and flowered fabrics in red, black, white, navy blue, and some other color I should find out the name of before I reopened Penny Thrift.

"How would you redecorate this?" I asked, taking her to the shelf next to the front door.

Virginia looked at me like I'd suggested rebellion. I reminded her Grandma wasn't going to walk through the front door. Ten minutes later, she'd left no pile untouched and even deemed some fabric as unsavable, but for Danny to play peek-a-boo with on the floor.

We moved to the next shelf and the next. After she'd rearranged the fabric in half the store, I returned to my initial question.

"Will you work for me?" I asked.

She shrugged and stooped down to pick up Danny.

"I don't quilt."

"Do you need to?"

"I can't sew my clothes fast enough to fill this store."

"I didn't expect you could."

"Then how am I helpful?"

Both she and Danny looked at me when she asked this question. They had the same eyes – same shade, same shape, same patience.

I looked at the quilt behind the register. Grandma's Flower Garden – I think that was the name of the pattern.

"Grandma told me she cut the pieces for this quilt from her mom's dresses the day her mom died. Her mother was the one who taught her how to sew and making a quilt from what she'd worn seemed like the best way to honor her memory."

I looked back at Virginia. "I don't know if you know much about my grandma, but she got pregnant young and married a man who ran off after my dad was born. It was a bad spot to be in, but she didn't change her habits until she woke up in a ditch a few years later."

I'd heard the story so often growing up it seemed more fable than true. The fact that it ended with Grandma seeing Jesus from the ditch didn't help. I'd mocked her about it last summer.

"Haven't I told you about the time Jesus found me in a ditch? No one else could have rescued me."

"You could have crawled out of that ditch," I argued.

"Sure, I could have crawled out of that ditch, eventually – once I could tell my head from my behind. But it would have only been a matter of time until I fell into another."

I get it. That's what I would tell Grandma if she was here. I get the ditch, though mine was a New York apartment. I get seeing the unseen. Mine hadn't taken the sharp outline of hers, but it was real to me all the same.

"She saw Jesus that morning and quit it all, cold turkey. She saved enough money from sewing and cooking to move out of her parents' house to this place, but she appreciated they hadn't tossed her out before then. They'd immigrated here for a better life, and she was their only daughter. Given the times and how small our town is, her choices would have made for a bit of a scandal. It'd make sense if they'd given up on her, but they took care of her until she could take care of herself. This quilt was her thank you."

I spread my arms and shrugged.

"I don't know why Grandma left this place to Ted and me. He's a carpenter. I'm a writer, not a seamstress or a businesswoman. I think there's some meddling on her part to keep me in this town, but I also think it's her way of taking care of me. The least I can do is try, but I'm not so disillusioned to think I can do what you just did."

Virginia looked confused. "Do what?"

I laughed.

"You rearranged half of her shop in the last hour. I loved it before, but I don't want to reopen and run it the same way she did. That'd be like pretending I'm her."

Virginia circled the shelves with Danny, looking over her work again and shuffling some of her choices.

"Okay," she said.

"Okay?"

I couldn't believe it. I exhaled, not realizing I'd been holding my breath.

"I don't have to quit my other job, right? I need the insurance."

"Keep the job. I can't pay you until we sell something, and I don't know when we're re-opening yet. Right now, I'm spending my days working on a project for my family's church, so I'll be here nights. How many hours do you think you can spare?"

"If I bring Danny, I could be here a couple nights a week and an afternoon on the weekends."

"I'll take it."

"And if I can't figure this out?" she asked.

I shrugged. "At least we tried. That's all Grandma ever asked of me anyway."

After Virginia and Danny left, I sat on the back stoop with the rooster napkins on my lap, tracing my fingers along the thick cotton thread. I'd been home almost two weeks, but I felt uncertain at every turn. It made the time seem longer. I didn't know what, if anything, was going to happen from trying to reopen the store, but I was looking forward to spending time here. For the first time since I'd returned, I felt like I had a reason to stay.

Then Ted called with another.

"Grace is in the hospital. Go now."

CHAPTER 14: LU

I've never traveled so quickly to a place I didn't want to be. I pushed past everything I hated about hospitals, even the things that have nothing to do with hospitals, like the sliding doors that admitted me to the front desk where I barked at the poor receptionist for Gracie's room number and then glared at her when she took ten seconds to find it. I ran to the elevator and woodpeckered the button until the doors opened and muttered about the elevator's snail speed, until it dinged me to the third floor.

I sprinted to Gracie's room. I heard her crying, I saw her curled on the bed, and I went to her. I released her hands from her knees and wrapped them around my neck, drawing out the sobs from her chest and shoulders.

We sat like this for a long time, her sobbing broken by conversation incoherent to anyone but us.

"I can't ..." she started without finishing.

"I'm here."

"And what if ..."

"We'll figure out what we need to figure out."

"The girls?"

"Ted is getting them – and why am I not on the school pick-up list? I'll take them after he gets here."

A light knock on the door and the doctor entered. Gracie's face was white as her pillowcase. She squeezed my hand, looking small and frightened and not ready to hear anything the doctor might have to say. I smiled at her and turned to the doctor, daring him with my eyes to tell us bad news.

He looked at Gracie. "Your baby girl is fine. You're fine. We're going to have to do a small procedure to keep your cervix closed, but even with this, you need to cut back on your activity. Not complete bed rest yet, but it could come to that. You've just started your third trimester – let's try to get you through as much of it as we can."

The news set Gracie crying again, and the doctor looked confused.

"This isn't bad news," he said.

"She's crying because you told her the baby is a girl."

"She doesn't want a girl?"

"She doesn't want to know. Look at her chart."

It was at this point – with Gracie sobbing and the doctor flipping through the paperwork, whispering, "I'm sorry," on repeat – that Ted entered the room.

He went straight to Gracie to take over the handholding.

"Tell me what happened," he whispered to her, surely expecting the worst.

"It's a girl," she wailed.

He leaned back. "You mean 'is' and not 'was?'"

Gracie nodded.

"And she's fine and you're fine?"

She nodded.

"Then why the hell are you crying and the doctor is apologizing?" Ted shouted.

"Because he wasn't supposed to tell me. And stop shouting."

The doctor looked like he was about to apologize again, but we needed to move this along. "They need a moment. You can come back in 15 minutes."

He obliged, and in the pause that followed, I realized I needed to do the same.

Ted reached across the bed for my hand. "Thank you, Lu."

"Where are the girls?" I asked.

"Neighbors. Mom and Dad won't be back until tomorrow."

"I'll stay with them tonight. You stay here."

My adrenaline took me to outside Gracie's door but no farther. I closed it before I slid down the wall to my heels. The vision of Gracie on the bed washed over me. I put my head in my arms and cried.

CHAPTER 15: JACKSON

I left the church as soon as I saw Ted's text. I hadn't seen him outside of church since Louisa went back to New York, and I was surprised to see his name flash across the screen. *Grace is in the hospital.* I didn't bother to grab my coat before I left.

I saw Louisa when I stepped off the elevator. She was crying. I went straight to her, leaned down, and put my hands on her shoulders.

"Louisa."

She looked at me, confused. "How'd you ..."

"Ted."

She nodded before leaning her head back and closing her eyes. She took a deep breath and wiped the tears from her cheeks. I gave her my hands to help her stand.

"Gracie is fine. The baby is fine. It's another girl, actually."

"Are you okay?"

Her tears started again, and I stood there with her, holding her hands until she could talk.

"I need to know why, Jackson," she whispered. "Please tell me why."

"Why what?"

"Why bad things happen to good people. Why, at the moment things seem hopeful, pain cuts in. Why God ..."

This wasn't the first time she asked these questions. Last year, I'd misinterpreted them as a search, but Louisa's questions, in particular the ones about God, led to nowhere. They were her constant doubts.

I dropped her hands.

"Louisa, I'm sorry, but I can't go around this again with you."

"Stop!" she shouted.

I took a step back – not from the volume, but from the anger in her eyes. Louisa stepped forward, canceling the space between us. She grabbed my hand and placed it on her heart. When she spoke again, her voice was low and insistent.

"What's it going to take, Jackson? You won't look at me. You don't talk to me. If you would give me the time of day, you might see something. I don't need you to prove anything; I believe all of it. But the person I love more than anyone else in this world was curled up on a bed in that hospital room. That image has memories for me, or have you forgotten that along with everything else?"

I looked at her hand holding mine to her chest. I felt her heart. My eyes met hers. She was waiting for an answer, but all I had was a question.

"What do you mean you believe all of it?" I asked.

She looked confused, but something that looked like relief followed. She tilted her head, keeping her eyes on mine. I knew I was in for it before she spoke.

"How about you answer my question first, Jackson."

I deserved that, and she deserved an apology, but not here, in the hospital hallway. I answered her first question instead.

"When I'm hurting, I read Psalm 39."

"Thank you."

She dropped my hand and left without another word.

I wanted to follow Louisa but couldn't. What just happened? What she said disoriented me enough that it took a minute to remember why I was here.

You came here to see Ted and Gracie, I reminded myself. I needed to get to it.

I walked into their room.

"Get into a fight with my sister, Jackson?" Ted asked.

"Sorry about that."

"Don't take it personally. She was yelling at the doctor when I arrived."

I laughed. "How come?"

"He was using words she didn't understand."

I laughed harder. Louisa was used to having the biggest vocabulary in the room.

"I think I messed up my words, too," I said.

Gracie looked at me. "You two needed a good fight. But you should still talk to her."

I nodded.

"And don't go empty-handed," she said.

I stayed at the hospital an hour longer than I meant to, but it'd been a long time since Ted, Gracie, and I had talked. We had a lot to catch up on. No one mentioned Louisa again, but she was on my mind. I had so many questions I wanted to ask her. I almost turned to go to her place when I left the hospital. Then I remembered Ted telling me she was watching the girls.

I went back to the church to get my coat and paused at the sanctuary doors. The construction crew would move in here next week. They needed to, at the very least, tear out the old burgundy carpet. My ex-wife, Kate, had complained about it before our wedding nine years ago.

"Can't we get married somewhere else?"

A week after our wedding, I would start seminary, and my mind was more focused on that than the wedding. My answer was no, regardless. This was my father's church. We would marry here.

And we did – on burgundy carpet that was slightly less stained than now. She was right about the carpet, but no one saw it because no one looked down. Everyone looked at her. To this day, nothing had come close to the sight of her walking down the aisle. Out of everything I hadn't seen about her and me, I saw that.

I was surprised the night I came home several years later and Kate was gone. I usually worked late, and she was rarely home when I got there. Didn't want to wait around for me, she'd said, but this time her stuff was gone, too. I circled our family room, empty except for a table and my books on the shelves by the fireplace. My chest tightened, making breathing hard, but I called her anyway.

"What's going on?"

"I've finally left you, Jackson."

"What do you mean 'finally?'"

"I mean I've been gone for years."

We'd never been great at fighting. Silence was easier, but her resentment had piled up. She chinked away at it now, starting at the beginning. She'd given up everything for me. When I went to seminary, she worked to support us. When I started pastoring for a small church in the middle of nowhere, she quit her job. When I wanted to start a family, she tried. When she miscarried, I turned back to my work, and she had nothing. I worked and worked. I put the church before her.

"You love the idea of me, of what I am to you, but you don't love me. You don't know me."

"I've known you since second grade. I've known since I was 15 that I would marry you. I told you on our first date, remember?"

"I'm not that girl anymore."

"You can't do this, Kate."

"No, you can't. No matter how bad things got between us, you wouldn't. I'm doing it for you."

I begged into the phone. It bought me two marriage counseling sessions, but I was still more concerned with saving face than saving us – or so Kate said when she filed for divorce.

She was right, but I didn't see it until after I'd lost everything. Half a year passed, and I was living at my grandparents' camp on the lake.

What's next?

I'd asked that question of God on repeat, but had no answer. One morning I stood on the dock with my Bible. I was the perfect picture of penitence except I wanted to chuck it in the water.

What now?

I opened it, expecting more silence. The words shouted from the page.

Meaningless, meaningless … everything is meaningless.

Ecclesiastes broke the silence. I thought it was God speaking to me about my life. A month later, I realized it was God telling me what I'd made of it. Kate had been right. I didn't know her. For years, I hadn't tried. I'd stayed, and would have always stayed with her, because I was her husband, but I had no idea what it meant to be a husband. After I decided Kate was who I'd marry, I'd moved on. Not with another woman, but with my life as I wanted it to be. I'd expected her to follow.

I called Kate. By this point, she had her own place, work, and life about two hours away from mine. She let me take her to lunch.

"You were right," I said as soon as the hostess sat us.

She laughed, not a nice one. "You don't change."

"What do you mean?"

"You can't stop yourself from leading with confession."

Her look told me I'd already said that. I wanted to go into further detail, but I changed the topic.

"Are you still going to church?" I asked.

"Only when I visit my parents. I'm not ready for a second round."

"Are you seeing anyone?"

She nodded. "You?"

"No."

The way I said it made her laugh again in the same way.

"I suppose that's for the best."

Kate smiled after she said it, maybe to soften the words, but it didn't matter. I knew what she meant. I bet she'd still say it, and after today, I wondered whether she was right about that, too.

It'd been nine years – seven married, a year after to grow up, and now a year back in Dunlap's Creek. Had I changed? Or, was I still that same man who saw and heard what was convenient?

I believe all of it.

With one sentence, Louisa had reoriented every interaction we'd had since she came back. She'd been trying to tell me this since that first Sunday morning. I could see that now. I closed my eyes and saw her angry ones. I could hear her words in this empty sanctuary.

What's it going to take, Jackson?

CHAPTER 16: LU

I collected the girls from the neighbors and decided to make something of our time and turn it into a sleepover at Aunt Lu's. We carried their sleeping bags across the yard and up the two flights to my bedroom. The attic caught their imagination as it had with mine as a little girl, and within a half hour, each niece had claimed a dormer window and built a fort around it, leaving me the whole bed and no covers. The girls slept great, but I wasn't used to their sleeping patterns. Every time they rolled over, I woke up and thought about Gracie until I fell back asleep. By the next morning, I doubted I'd slept more than ten consecutive minutes. I gave up and tiptoed downstairs to make coffee.

I opened my Bible to Psalm 39. By the end of the second verse, I could see why Jackson suggested it. The honesty ripped down the page, ending with: *Look away from me, that I may rejoice again before I depart and am no more.* I didn't know you were allowed to tell God to go away, but pain has a way of pushing out the polite. It swallows platitudes. All that's left is what's there, ugly or not. We say what we say, even psalmists. I empathized.

My first caffeine round did little for my energy, and I'd just filled the hotpot when I heard the screen door open behind me.

It was Jackson. Even after everything, my instinct was to go to him. I wanted to wrap my arms around him. I'd never done it, but I knew how it'd feel. I could smell it, taste it. It was right there.

Self-control comes in many forms. For my part, it looked like staying where I was and hearing what Jackson had to say.

"I'm sorry, Louisa."

"Jackson, I'm ..."

"No," he interrupted, stepping forward and holding up his hand. "Your leaving doesn't excuse how I've treated you since you've been back. You've tried to talk to me, and I've shut you down every time. There's no reason for it other than …"

He faltered, and as much as I wanted to get on with my apology, I wanted him to finish his sentence. There were important words in there. I silently completed the space with the ones I wished he'd use.

In the end, he shrugged. "Can we call it self preservation and leave it at that?"

No.

My mind responded so vehemently; I'm amazed my lips didn't form the word. If we weren't going to lay out our past, I didn't know how to move on with him, but Jackson's next question cut into further deliberation on my part.

"What happened in New York?"

I'd been waiting for someone to ask me that question ever since I'd come back. I'd wanted it to be him. I rubbed the back of my neck, looking at him.

"I want to tell you, but I can't. Even under the best of circumstances, I can't seem to talk about it, and I'm exhausted now. I barely slept last night."

"That's why I'm making you coffee," he said. His smile was a living memory, as was the paper bag he produced from behind his back. It held a stove-top espresso, and he was going to make some for me like he had last Thanksgiving. He crossed the kitchen and started unloading his bag next to me.

"I haven't used this in months," he said. "Take your time."

"How old are those beans?" I asked, the nostalgia cut by my concern over whether he was using stale ones from last fall.

He laughed. "I see some things haven't changed. I picked them up last night."

"In anticipation you'd eat crow this morning?"

"And that you'd need a little incentive to start talking. Now get to it."

I sat at the kitchen table and started at the beginning, how my first week in New York I'd walked a circuit that ended each day at a cement bench outside a small church near John's apartment. I told him about the first Sunday I'd gone to church and how Pastor Eddy sat me down in the front pew before preaching like a sword – no anecdotes, no humor – just words from the Bible and why we should believe them.

I told him how I became a student of sorts, reading about apologetics and taking notes.

"I would talk about it all with John. I played you; he played me. It wasn't long before I saw the truth of what you'd preached last year – the chase behind the chase for meaning. For the first time, I saw how God could be that answer, but I didn't believe it."

Jackson placed a demitasse in front of me and took the seat next to me. I picked up the small white mug and inhaled.

I smiled at him. "Think you've still got it?"

"Not to make too big of a deal, but I feel like our friendship hinges on how well I made this espresso."

Jackson smiled. I would have made this moment last all day, but that's the problem with espresso. It comes in a tiny cup. I sipped, and the roast landed, searing a bitter trail along my tongue and throat. I followed it with another inhale, no sip this time. The combination of taste and smell might do for me what a bad night's sleep couldn't.

"Well done," I affirmed.

Jackson leaned back in his chair.

"Finish your story. When did belief kick in?"

"Ironically, with John. Aside from Eddy, he was the only person I talked to about this, despite him being the one person in my life who could not care less. Whether God existed was irrelevant to him, though his life had taken a turn, too. Working in a New York law firm is hard. He was doing well, but he was losing himself. I think he saw me as the missing factor. In his mind, everything would be fine if I stayed with him."

I'd avoided thinking about my last night in New York since I'd returned home, but it was waiting for me. I'd needed to make a move – either out on my own or in with John. I wanted to want the latter. I thought sleeping with him would make that work. It didn't, but what undid me was what he'd said.

For me, there's you. I just want you. I don't care about the rest of this. I'd give it all up for you.

John had wanted me to save him, and his desperation triggered my own. I saw I was drowning, had always been, and would always be. I couldn't do for another what I couldn't do for me. I couldn't save myself.

"Louisa?"

Jackson's voice startled me from memory. It took me a second to register the tears filling my eyes.

"I'm remembering what happened that night."

"Do you want to …?"

"I can't talk about John." I took a deep breath, trying to get my emotions under control. "But I want to finish this if you're still willing to hear it."

He nodded.

"In everything that happened last year – losing Grandma Pat, losing my job – I'd never questioned my ability to keep trying and make something of it, but when John presented me with the idea of being his happiness there was no question. I couldn't be that. I wasn't my own happiness. It was impossible. Once I saw that, everything fell in line, and Mark 5:24 made perfect sense."

"What's that?" Jackson asked.

"Mark 5:24."

"Remind me what that says."

"You're a pastor. How can you not know this passage?"

He put his fingertips together. "It's time I told you something."

"What?"

"I don't have the whole Bible memorized."

I put my hands to my chest, unable to keep the smile from my face.

"It's the story of the bleeding woman touching Jesus' cloak. I'd read it earlier that day, and it read like everything else in the Bible – a strange story that was supposed to have something to do with me. I remember tossing it on the kitchen table, feeling let down, again, that the Bible brought more distance than answers.

"Then the day happened, another day of trying and failing, but in such a big way this time. It was too big for me to get around. When I read the story of the bleeding woman again that night, I was in it. It was my story, and I was her. I was the woman who had tried for years to heal herself, but it was a patch job. I needed to touch Jesus. It was the only way to stop the bleeding."

I'd never spoken this thought aloud, and I wondered if it landed strange, but Jackson had leaned in, his eyes following my words. It helped me say the rest of them.

"Jesus became real. I stayed awake the rest of the night reading my Bible. I saw myself in every story. I saw how Jesus had been speaking to me all of my life. It gave me the courage to come back here."

"Why did you need courage?" Jackson asked.

I put my chin in my hands and looked at the table. I'd told my story true, but I hadn't told him all of it, like how I'd missed him every day I was gone. How I'd written him a stack of letters, unsent and sitting right now in my room upstairs. How hearing about him moving on made me realize I hadn't.

I needed the courage to face you.

He didn't say anything to break the silence, and I took another minute, weighing the risk of my honesty – not for my sake, but for his. I looked at him.

"Are you happy, Jackson?"

He looked confused. "Why do you ask?"

"Because I'm sorry about how I left. If I could go back …"

"Don't do that."

"What?"

"Run through your past like it controls your present. God doesn't hold it against you. I don't either. And in answer to your question, yes. I'm happy."

He looked like he meant it. He sounded like he meant it.

So, I lied.

"I needed the courage to make tough choices, to leave a job I liked and to leave John. I had the makings of a good life in New York. There are no promises for me here."

"Do there need to be?"

"No." I stood up to take my mug to the sink. "I don't plan to leave again, though I'm not yet sure why I'm here."

I washed his espresso maker, handed him back his paper bag, and walked him to the back door.

"Isn't this the part where you say, 'Welcome to the Kingdom,' or something like that?" I asked.

Jackson threw back his head back and laughed so loudly I shushed him. I still had five more minutes before I needed to get my nieces ready for school.

"Maybe a few years ago," he said. "How about now, I just say I'm glad you're back."

He opened the door but turned to me before leaving.

"I missed you."

I nodded. Behind his statement was closure. Whatever had passed between us last year was done, and his forgiveness wrapped it tidy with a bow. Jackson had moved on.

I smiled a smile I didn't feel and waved goodbye. Better that than risk giving voice to a longing far from gone.

CHAPTER 17: LU

Getting the girls ready for school took an army, except it was just me this morning. It wasn't until Holly sprinted to her preschool class from the car that I saw the bird's nest in the back of her head. *Brush hair*, I mentally added to the morning list. *And teeth*. I'd forgotten that, too, but do three-year-olds have morning breath? I wasn't about to call her back for a smell check.

Mine was minty fresh, though. If I'm reduced to one act of morning vanity, tooth brushing is it, and it was the one minute I'd had since waking up my nieces, which is why I was stuffing my curls into a ponytail as I walked down the silent church hallway. The early school start put me to work before the construction crew, but the silence amplified my jitters. I was nervous to see Jackson.

A murmur of Christmas music playing from what sounded like a record greeted me as I descended the basement steps. It grew louder as I walked down the hallway. I pushed open the double doors of my space to find the cinder block walls covered in colored Christmas lights of all shapes and sizes, held with duct tape. In the corner stood a sad Christmas tree that made Charlie Brown's look fancy.

It was Jackson's handiwork, and I pointed my finger at him when he came down awhile later.

"This Christmas display is re-enforcing my prejudice against this place," I said.

"Which is?"

"It's the birthplace of Jack the Ripper."

He laughed and put his hands in his pockets, as he leaned against the doorway. "I thought the music would add a cheerful touch, but it does sound eerie."

"I'm expecting headless Nutcracker dolls to emerge any time. Did you do all this before you came to my house this morning?"

"Last night."

My face must have shown my surprise.

"I was nervous," he said. "Jingle Bells cut the edge."

"What if we hadn't worked it out?"

"I'd have asked those headless nutcracker dolls to clean up before you got here."

"Can I turn the music off now?"

"Please. And let me know if you need any help," he said and walked back down the hallway.

I did need help, but it wasn't until I began hanging snowflake decals that I clued into the source of my procrastination. Instead of Jackson's office, I went to his dad's. I'd checked in over the last couple weeks, asking clarification questions that were more of a stalling tactic than anything. The 50th anniversary was at the end of June, and I needed a rough draft before the end of May, leaving me with a little over a month.

I'd unpacked every box that first week and organized the contents topically. This past week I'd created a few outlines. The first was chronological, but that started to feel like a yearbook without an end. I didn't know what not to include, and including everything would mean volumes that no one, including me, would read.

Then, I tried organizing chapters by various mission statements the church had adopted over the years, but this felt like a series of press releases. It also pushed me to using churchy language I didn't understand and didn't like. Was "missional" a legitimate word? I wasn't sure, but it was one of the church's core values 10 years ago.

Basically, I was in one of the worst places a writer could be with a big project, a tight deadline, no starting place, and no inspiration. I knocked on Paul's door. He looked up from his desk.

Can I quit? I wanted to ask. Instead I said, "I need some help."

"Take a seat. I'll fetch you some coffee."

He was up and back before I could tell him not to bother. I placed the Styrofoam cup on his desk, turning it in half circles as I explained my different approaches.

"Or maybe since the church has had three pastors, I should tell it through their perspectives?" I added, having just come up with that idea.

Paul shook his head. He didn't want the book to center around their efforts.

"I don't like any of my ideas," I summarized. "And I'm worried I'm the wrong person for this."

Paul sat back in his chair now, crossing his arms. He was never quick to respond, and when he did, it was with a question.

"What are your church memories?" he asked.

I opened my mouth to answer, but my filter kicked in. I stayed quiet.

"What?" he asked.

I shook my head.

He leaned onto his desk. "There's this perception that pastors can't handle what people have to say. But do you know what we do between one Sunday and the next? We hear what people say. Trust me, people don't hold back, especially when it comes to how they feel about Sunday mornings."

He smiled. "Now tell me. What are your memories of going to church when you were younger?"

I pushed away the coffee I'd been not sipping and sat back in my chair.

"I never liked going to church."

"Why?"

"The Saturday night bath. The stiff dresses on Sunday morning. The recitations followed by sitting and listening. I felt half-starved by the time the communion cracker came around. When I got older, all I saw was hypocrisy – people nodding like they believed on Sunday but not acting like it come Monday morning."

Paul started laughing halfway through my confession. It gave me courage to say the real one.

"My complaints became more a question of belief. Even though I came to church last year, I didn't feel like I belonged."

Paul didn't flinch. I guess it was naive to think I'd said anything he hadn't heard before.

"Jackson's sermons got better after you came back last summer."

"What do you mean?"

"There's a stereotype for preacher's kids. They believe or rebel. Jackson was in the first group. He was a good kid. He always believed in God – not without thought, but without question. He preached from that point-of-view, assuming everyone would fall in line. After his divorce, I thought he'd preach to more of the tension we have with faith, that it's not absent of doubt, but his sermons were as adamant as ever. Then you showed up. What did you do?"

"It's a coincidence. I didn't do anything."

"Nothing?"

I rewound the months, trying to remember why I'd come to church in the first place. It wouldn't have been my idea, but I'd run into Jackson at Ted's baseball game and then again at a wedding and then I remembered what happened at that wedding.

I laughed.

"Your son might be a good pastor's kid, but he's tricky. We ran into each other at a wedding. He tricked me into eating cake with him, and then he ate half of mine. He asked good questions. He listened to me. I felt like he was the first person to 'see' me after I returned from New York, so when he asked me to come to church, I did. I came early enough that I heard him practicing, and ...." I stopped.

"I guess I did do something," I said.

"What?"

"I told him no one would listen to his sermon if he started the way he'd planned."

"Which was?"

"'Open your Bible to Ecclesiastes,'" I mimicked in my best Jackson voice.

Paul laughed.

"I guess that's where it all started for me," I concluded.

"It started for you long before, Lu."

I shook my head. "I came with my family as a kid, but I'm new to all of this."

"All those years of wishing the communion cracker was bigger weren't for nothing." Paul left his chair behind the desk to sit next to me. "It doesn't matter what brings us here on Sundays. God will have his way. Take you, for example. You didn't come here that first Sunday intending anything, but through you, Jackson's preaching sharpened. He's reaching a new audience now. It's not just people looking for a new church, it's people who wouldn't intend to go to church, like you."

Paul stood and rummaged through desk until he found the church bulletin. He took a pen from his shirt pocket and circled several items before handing it over to me.

"Get out of the basement next week and go to where the people are instead."

His circles were more socializing than I did in a year if I could help it.

"I'd prefer to hang out in the basement."

"I know you would. I'm a quiet person, too. But the church is people."

I sighed, but I stood to do as instructed.

"Don't forget your coffee," he said before I left. I turned, wondering how honest I should be. Then I remembered we were in between Sundays and hearing what people really have to say was Paul's main job.

"I like coffee, but not that coffee."

"I was wondering when you were going to say that."

"I have two French presses. Maybe I could bring one to keep here?"

"So long as you share."

"Not many people like my coffee, including Jackson," I warned him.

He opened the door for me. "No one's perfect."

When I picked up Holly from preschool it took her 15 minutes to put on her seatbelt "all by myself."

I tried to help.

She screamed.

I decided my patience could outlast my eardrums.

By the time I started the car, we were both hungry, so we stopped for lunch. Lunch included three nibbles of chicken fingers between three false-alarm potty breaks, the last of which turned into a meet-and-greet with a preschool friend who invited her to the playground. My ears were still ringing from the last time I crossed Holly, so off to the playground we went, which used to be a strip of dirt with one metal slide and three squeaky swings. They were death traps, but way more fun than the bright plastic contraptions these girls could barely gain traction on.

I wanted to read a book on the bench, but all the other moms were chatting in clusters. I played good aunt and engaged with the mom I'd met at lunch. She carried the conversation from the first hello.

I was so good with kids, did I have any? No, well maybe my husband and I would someday. Oh, no husband? Sometimes it takes a while for the right man to come along.

I didn't have to ask how she'd met her man. She offered up the tale, which carried us until pick-up time for my older nieces. My parents had come home early, and I dropped the girls there for an after school snack while I crossed the yard to Gracie's.

"Why don't your girls ride the bus?" I asked, lying down next to her in bed. The hospital had released her mid-morning, and I figured she'd had enough rest to deal with hearing about my day.

"The bad language."

"It can't be worse than the conversation I had at the playground with Julie, mom of Riley."

"Playground chats are the worst," Gracie agreed, closing her eyes.

"Especially when your husband and child resume is blank." I nudged Gracie from the beginnings of her nap. "What's going on with you?"

"I guess my cervix was injured with Holly, and I'm lucky something didn't happen sooner. The plan now is what the doctor said – rest or early birth."

She kept her eyes closed, and it was hard for me to read how she was feeling. I held her hand.

"And your day before the playground?" she asked a few minutes after I thought she'd fallen asleep.

I told her about making up with Jackson, Christmas decorations, and my forthcoming church field trips. I ended with Paul's assessment.

"According to Paul, my whole purpose for being here last year was to 'sharpen Jackson's preaching.'"

She laughed – her first. "I bet you loved that."

"It's the role I've always wanted to play."

"Men are stupid sometimes. Did you tell Jackson how you feel?"

"No."

Her look told me women are stupid sometimes, too.

"I am not messing with that man," I said.

"He's making decisions without all of the information at hand. Tell him."

"Says the married lady."

"At one point, I had to tell your brother how I felt."

"Did he ever have to tell you?"

"No, he's always made that plain."

"Then what was the risk?"

Gracie changed the topic.

"I know there's enough to be upset about with this incompetent cervix thing, but here's what gets me. I had two months, and it felt like something that would be mine before the next baby came. The clock reset yesterday, plus two months of bed rest. I can't even take care of my girls.

"Do you think I'm a horrible, selfish person?" she asked, turning to me and gripping my hand.

"You're running this question by me?"

"You're not horrible and selfish. Look at what you're doing with Jackson."

"You think that's cowardly, not selfless."

She smiled, not denying it.

"Tell me about the plans you'd made for the next two months," I said.

She moved her hands from mine and placed them like a pillow under her cheek. I did the same.

"I wanted to stop watching home renovation shows and fix up a room of my own. There's a group of women I've known for a long time at church, and we always see one another, but with our kids. I thought I'd have them all over to dinner, but just the moms and have Ted take the kids all afternoon, too, so I could cook a real dinner. I wanted to paint my fingernails one morning and not care the polish would chip by nighttime. You're always reading, and I can't remember the last time I read. I thought I might finish a book. I thought about getting a part-time job. How stupid is that? I mean, no one is looking to hire a pregnant lady in her third trimester. What would it be like to work somewhere and be Gracie – not the girls' mom, not Ted's wife – but Gracie. Not that I can get away from all of that in a town this small. It was nice to think about, though."

Her tears started, but different this time. Less fearful and more regretful. She took my hands again.

"What's the point, Lu?"

It was tempting to spin the moment. We could start moving through her list. I could paint her nails right now and hand her a book to read while they dried. Then I remembered Psalm 39 from this morning and what it said about pain. Sometimes the kindest response was to let the emotions run through. I didn't give her the footnote, and I didn't leave the bed to get the nail polish. I remembered the verses for her, like I would remember her list, keeping it until the right time.

CHAPTER 18: LU

The best part of the next week was the new coffee shop. Dunlap's Creek is a small town an hour away from anything resembling a city. It's easy to think the town will be as it has always been, so small changes are noticeable, like hanging baskets around the town square and the coffee shop in the old train depot. I went on Monday as a lark, and each successive day as a coping mechanism. Visits to the knitting church club, where discussion of precancerous moles took center stage, and the church playgroup – a shriek fest – will do that. By Thursday I was rattled. Virginia called to say she couldn't come to Penny Thrift that night because Danny was sick. I decided to take the night off, too, and texted Mom I'd be home for dinner.

I smelled the pot roast when I opened the front door. Mom's no cook, but she can cook this one thing, and the smell radiates to every corner of the house. My mind registered "gravy," and I headed to the kitchen to help. The dining room set for four stopped me. Was that my parents' wedding china on the table? The doorbell rang and suspicion set in.

The smile Mom flashed me didn't help.

"Do you want to get it?" she asked.

"No."

"Don't you want to see who it is?"

"No."

"I prepared this nice dinner."

"I'm ready to eat it, Mom." The door between the kitchen and dining room was still swinging, releasing wafts of roast at steady intervals. I wiped the saliva from the sides of my mouth. "I'm not interested in a replay."

I was referring to last summer when Grandma Pat had staged a similar set-up.

"I didn't invite Jackson," she defended.

"So, it is a set-up!"

"Not if you don't open the door it's not."

I crossed my arms; Mom put her hands on her hips. My stomach grumbled. It would have to wait. I was not opening that door.

Dad's coming down the stairs cut the stalemate. Mom smiled at me before joining her proxy to greet the man I would meet in about 30 seconds. I stayed where I was, for no reason other than it was the ground I had left.

Mom returned to the dining room guest and frowned at me – a frown that meant "smile," and I did. It wasn't this guy's fault I was single, and my mom thought it was a problem. I knew he wouldn't be the one to fix it. His hand felt like a dead fish in mine, and he was half a head shorter than me.

His name was Alex Sams, and Mom had met him at a planning commission meeting. Bike routes to the schools were on the agenda, and Alex was our new city planner.

"And I thought 'Why not have you over to dinner?'" she summarized. "Especially since you're about the same age as Lu."

It was a nice gesture for what now felt like a play date. I knew my role and started asking questions to finish what Mom started.

"Where are you from?" I asked Alex.

"St. Louis."

"Did you buy a place here?"

"On Vine Street."

"Are you the one responsible for the pretty hanging baskets around the town square?"

"No."

We sat at the table, and I went for an open-ended question, hoping to cajole a few more words out of the man.

"What do you think about Dunlap's Creek so far?"

"I like it."

I looked at him and silently counted to five. He met my quiet with quiet. Dad picked up the slack with a question about Alex's family. Three names, no further details. Mom asked if they were in St. Louis, too. He said, "Yes."

She looked to me to ask the next question, and we volleyed like this through the pot roast, eating it in record time. I shoveled down the hot fudge sundae Mom brought out after dinner. I wasn't hungry for it, but I needed Alex to do the same and go home. He sat there, staring at the sundae.

"Too full?" I asked.

"Lactose intolerant."

I wiped the sundae from around my mouth, waiting to see if he'd offer up a background story to close out the night. He didn't.

"Well now we'll know for …" I was about to say "next time" but there wasn't going to be one of those, at least not without several more people to carry the conversation.

My unfinished sentence made a fitting end to an awkward evening. I finished my sundae and stood. He stood. I walked him to the door, and he left. I checked my watch. Longest hour ever.

Mom and I cleared the table in silence. There was a lot to say, but I was too exhausted to say it. After we brought the last load from the table, we looked at each other. Then we started laughing.

"I won't do it again," she promised.

I nodded.

"And I'll do the dishes," she offered as a handshake to our peace treaty.

I believed her. So, I knew what happened the next afternoon wasn't my mother's handiwork.

"Is six okay for tonight?" Jackson shouted as I walked by his office.

I had no idea what he was talking about, and I had a minute to find out before my next meeting. I back tracked and poked my head in his office.

"What?"

"Gracie asked me to dinner tonight but didn't say a time. You know about this, right?"

Shaking my head would make this worse. I nodded.

"Yes, dinner is at six," I said.

"And you're making soup? I didn't think you cooked."

"Gracie told you I'm making soup?"

"She did."

"Then I guess I am."

"Can I ask a favor?"

"So long as it's not to cook something else. Chicken noodle soup is the one thing I know how to make."

"The soup sounds great. Can I bring Rebecca? She's doesn't know a ton of people in town yet, and being with your family is …"

"Like playing a game of whack-a-mole," I finished for him.

"I was going to say they're great."

"Bring Rebecca. We'll let her decide."

CHAPTER 19: JACKSON

"Tell me about her family again," Rebecca said as I opened the car door. She was normally up for anything, but she hesitated saying yes to this dinner. I heard it in her voice on the phone. The half hour it took me to wrap up work and pick her up hadn't helped.

She settled in the seat, and instead of going around to the driver's side, I sat back on my heels – our eyes now level – and covered her hands with mine.

"Nervous?"

She nodded.

"We're doing this so you can see you don't have to be."

"What if they don't like me?"

"Do they need to?"

"What if she doesn't like me?"

"Louisa will like you."

"And that's another thing. Everyone calls her Lu. Except you. What am I supposed to call her?"

"It doesn't matter. Do you know what does?"

Did she know she was gripping my hands?

"You do. You matter to me. I don't have any control over Louisa working at the church, but if I can do anything to help you feel better about it, I will. If you'd rather stay in tonight, that's fine. I'll call and cancel."

She leaned her head against the headrest, looking at me. After a little while, she smiled.

"I'd feel better if we brought Roddy or something."

I laughed. "You have to be the one person who thinks bringing Roddy into this would be helpful."

"I like him."

I put my hand to my chest in mock hurt. "Should I be concerned now?"

"No."

She leaned over and kissed me.

Louisa's nieces rushed Rebecca as she came through the door, and Ted was the first adult to find us.

"Feel free to take one of these girls home with you, Rebecca," he said, after peeling them off to play outside. "We've made another."

"They're not replaceable parts, Ted," Gracie said from the couch. I leaned down to hug her and Rebecca sat next to her. The two descended into baby talk I couldn't track. I followed Ted through the dining room – nodding to Nana Bea, who sat at the table – and back to the kitchen. Louisa stood over a pot, an odd sight.

"You have Lu to thank for tonight's soup and me for making it taste good," Ted said.

She rolled her eyes.

"Because you butt in per usual, Ted."

"I had to move things along," he told me in between bites of a carrot he stole from her cutting board. "She invited Roddy here for lunch the other weekend, and at the rate she was adding salt, the man would still be here."

"There are worse people to bring around," I said, thinking how Roddy would find my defense amusing.

"She took him to church, too."

"He took me," Louisa corrected.

"And here's the kitchen," Louisa's mom said, taking Rebecca on a tour of the downstairs.

"It smells great in here," Rebecca said, smiling at Louisa.

"What are your thoughts on taking people to church?" Louisa asked Rebecca, not responding to the compliment or the smile.

"I don't think it's a bad idea."

Louisa turned back to Ted, the look on her face claiming victory.

"What do you think about taking people like Roddy to church?" he asked Rebecca.

Louisa's dad walked in from the deck, saving Rebecca from getting any further in the middle.

"Well now, Jackson," he said, "it's nice to see you here again, and I'm glad you brought Rebecca."

By the time he was done making small talk with her, Louisa and Ted were ready to play nice. Mark Sokolowski had that effect on people. He was good man.

All of us were more than willing to let tonight's dinner play out according to the nieces' agenda, which were strings of questions directed at Rebecca. Did she have sisters? If she had a cat (she didn't) would she want it to be white or brown? Would she name it 'Peacock?

Rebecca met their enthusiasm. She was as curious about them as they were about her, giving the rest of us plenty of time to eat our first bowl of soup without incident. I was starting my second bowl when Abigail asked the one question I should have anticipated from a girl who dressed in princess costumes more often than not.

"How did you and Pastor Jackson start dating?"

I looked at Louisa. If she had any reaction to the question, her face didn't show it.

"Don't you remember?" Rebecca said, turning the question back to Abigail. "It was in your Sunday school class."

Abigail shook her head.

"A paint bomb exploded," I said, catching up. I put my arm around Rebecca, rubbing her shoulder. "My dad was preaching, so I went downstairs to see what you kids were up to."

"Do you go to this church?" Rebecca had shouted to me from inside a classroom. I was pretty sure I hadn't seen her before, but it was hard to tell. There was paint all over her face.

I nodded as one of the kids in her class shouted, "Hey, Pastor Jackson!"

She laughed. "The pastor! Could you take over for a bit while I clean myself up?"

When she came back a minute later, she picked up the lesson like nothing had happened. I stayed, in case she needed more help. The preschool room was a case of barely organized crazy, but Rebecca made it fun. I was as disappointed as the kids when it was over. I stayed to clean up.

"How'd you get roped into this?"

"I'm new in town and Nicole was the first person I met in the teacher's lounge. She invited me to church and then called last night that they were short-staffed down here and asked if I could help."

"You might never get the paint out of your shirt."

"I'm more concerned about my hair," she said, holding up a clump streaked in green paint. "I'm actually blonde."

I knew. I'd been looking, and I'd had more fun in the last hour than I'd had in the last month. I asked Rebecca to lunch without thinking.

"I don't go out with pastors," she said.

I was familiar with that push back and backtracked.

"Oh, well …"

"Jackson, I'm kidding. Give me a minute to wash out my hair."

"The goal was to put the finger paint on the paper, but one girl thought it would look good in her hair, which set off a chain reaction," Rebecca explained, and the conversation moved on from there.

After dinner, Ted coached a baseball game in the backyard. It was as good a time as I'd ever had here, but tonight felt like a reverse instead of a step forward. After I dropped Rebecca off, I realized something else. I hadn't talked to Louisa once the whole evening.

CHAPTER 20: LU

"Do people try to set you up?" I asked Roddy.

His look told me he didn't need help. He didn't, even today when he was incognito with a ball cap and sunglasses. It was Saturday afternoon, and he was hung over from the night before – or so he'd warned me when I'd called early this morning to see if he'd go on a field trip with me. He hadn't put up a fight when I suggested we take my car.

"I didn't know there were bookstores anymore," Roddy said, his first comment in the half hour we'd been in the car.

"They're scarce, but I need to get out of town, and I need some inspiration."

Bookstores, libraries, any place with books were a sort of mother ship for me. I still carried my public library card for New York City. The glove compartment in my car was stuffed with paperbacks to read at train stops. In my purse right now was a book I'd started reading with Caroline. Gracie had finished it with her in one of our many kid swaps this week, but I wanted to know how it ended.

"If you wanted inspiration, you should have come out with me last night."

"This is inspiration for the church anniversary book. How much of your last night would have applied?"

"Keep to the topic too much, and you're risking dull. Don't you worry about that?"

For more than the church book, I almost replied. I asked about his work instead. He was overseeing the construction on an apartment complex in a college town a couple counties away. It was running a month behind schedule but fully leased for the start of the academic year in August. It didn't seem to bother him. Right now, he was dozing in and out like he had nothing on his mind.

"My project has a lot less on the line. Why are you less stressed than me?" I asked him.

"I've been here before, Lu. We always get it done; we just have to make choices."

"Like whether to include indoor plumbing?"

He laughed. "Let me know when your time at the church is up, and I'll hire you."

"By then I should have Penny Thrift running."

"And where are we with that?"

I smiled at his use of "we" because unlike the church book, which was on me, Penny Thrift was a group project with Virginia on design and me on the re-open, the marketing and promotion of which was familiar, given my work on the wedding expo last year. The business side also felt doable because Roddy was a text away. This was the first time I'd seen him since he'd had lunch at my house, but I'd texted him dozens of times since with questions. His return messages were quick, pointed, and without charm. The Roddy on the other side of a text was my favorite Roddy.

As soon as we walked down the inspirational fiction aisle at the bookstore, I wished I hadn't brought him. I wished I hadn't brought me, but how was I to know what I would find?

"I don't understand," I whispered, barely hearing myself because Roddy was laughing loudly enough to turn heads.

I reached for the nearest book – slow and hesitant, not afraid it would bite, but rather wishing it would. When I picked it up, the woman on the cover didn't change her expression. She was too intent on looking into the distance, across the prairie. Fields are windy places, and the photo showed a gust catching a tendril from her bun, yet her bonnet looked secure. *Love Comes Around.* That was the title.

"But what does it mean?" I whispered.

I put the book back and scanned the rest of the covers on the shelf, but it was an unbroken horizon of fields, historic costumes, and titles with more adjectives and adverbs than was healthy. Roddy was still laughing. I elbowed his side.

"Are you done?" I asked.

"Are you?"

At least his retort required him to take a breath.

"I don't understand," I repeated, shuffling through the stacks like a woman searching for an obscure size in a sample sale.

"Let me break it down for you." He paused. "You're Amish."

I looked at the evidence in front of me. The nearest book featured a woman wearing a high-necked collar. I backed out of the aisle. Then I bee-lined it out of the store.

"What are you doing?" Roddy called from behind me.

"Giving up."

"You're not giving up."

He picked up three books, bought them, and presented the bag to me at the front of the store. It swung left and right, looking like a harmless thing.

I ignored the offering and walked to the car. Once we were seated, I popped open the glove compartment, showing him the books. I pulled the one from my purse and waved it in front of his face. When I sat, I remembered the one in my back pocket and tossed it on his lap. In the trunk, there was also the paper bag I'd filled with books when I was supposed to be helping Virginia buy fabrics at a garage sale earlier this week.

"I think you have a problem," he concluded.

"No, I have a passion. When you need to let off steam, you do it in a way that requires you to wear sunglasses the next day. I read. I read because I enjoy it. Sometimes I read to escape. And other times I read to make sense of something."

I sighed, leaning my head against the seat.

"My family tried to set me up twice this week. Once with a guy who doesn't talk and the second time with Jackson because that worked so well with him and me before."

I had more to say, but Roddy had started laughing.

"Why would they do that?" he asked.

"Well, one, they're my family."

"And Jackson came?"

"He brought Rebecca."

Roddy laughed harder. "Did she bring brownies?"

"No." I closed my eyes and saw them across the table from me, a sight I'd tried to avoid for most of dinner, but one could stare at her chicken noodle soup for only so long. The first time I looked over, Jackson's arm was around Rebecca. The second time, his arm was back to his side, but he was looking at her. I opened my eyes to stop the memory.

"I bet she's a good church girl and owns all the books in that bag."

I turned to look at Roddy, appreciating that he'd gone quiet. His face showed no reaction to what I'd said, and he was still wearing his sunglasses. The combination worked for me, creating a neutral space to say what I'd been sensing since I came back.

"I used to think the distance between me and the people closest to me was a question of belief, but I've come to the same answers as them, and I still don't fit. I don't know how to be back here. I don't know how to be a changed person in a place that sees me as I was, and I'm starting to question whether this change is all in my head. I was hoping today for a story to help me out. I was hoping the story would help me tell the story of the church. I was hoping writing the story of the church would help me see where I could fit into it."

He opened his mouth, but I cut him off.

"I swear, if you tell me I can solve this problem by strutting around town in a little black dress, I'm going to toss these books at your head."

He nodded and laid his hand on my shoulder.

"Lu, I don't think the books can handle that kind of violence. It would shock them."

I didn't want to, but I laughed again.

"Can we please leave now?" he asked.

I nodded and started the car.

"And you'll stop talking?"

I smiled and turned on the radio.

Though Roddy had been helping me with Penny Thrift, he'd never seen the place, and we decided to stop there on the way back to his house. He fell asleep less than ten minutes into the drive and didn't wake up when I parked. I opened the windows so he wouldn't stifle and headed in.

After I'd gone through the numbers that first week, I'd questioned whether we needed the store at all. Online sales had outpaced store sales over the last couple years. It would make sense to close the actual shop, and I'd texted Roddy about it.

"Close or continue?"

"Or run the store differently," he'd responded.

One thing I'd seen in working with him was how he rarely thought in binaries. Roddy thought in possibilities. Running the store as a place to shop didn't make much sense when people didn't really go to places to shop anymore, but what else could this place be? Virginia and I talked about the answers to that question as we'd traveled to garage sales and thrift stores over the last couple weeks, searching for fabric. The more we talked around the question, the more I saw I had choices. The mortgage was paid, the utilities were minimal. There was no financial need to close or limit it to a storage facility, and neither of these options excited me. Re-opening was a lot of effort anyway, so why not try something different? We could use the store for anything.

For what, I still didn't know, but it meant redesigning the space so it was less fabric-centric. After a couple brainstorming sessions with Ted, we decided to move most of the inventory to the basement, using the best as decoration and inspiration along the walls. This would leave the middle open for anything. I'd wanted him to install a few skylights to bring more light in, but Ted told me no – too expensive. Virginia asked him to pull up the old carpet and refinish the wood floors underneath, and he said yes since the stain was cheap and the sweat equity was on him.

Today was for clearing out. Virginia had left Danny with a friend, and we were both ready to put in a full afternoon. The floor was filled with empty boxes, piles to keep, and piles to go. She had the music playing when I got there. Classic rock. I turned it up. We worked quickly, boxing up the largest bookshelf by the end of the hour. It wasn't until I headed to the kitchen for a glass of water that I remembered about Roddy in the car and that was because he now stood in the doorway. He didn't say anything, and he wasn't looking at me. His sunglasses were off, and he was looking at Virginia.

She noticed him a second later. I turned down the music to make introductions.

"Virginia, this is …"

"I know him," she said, cutting me off. They looked at each other for a few more seconds before she said she needed something from the basement and went downstairs.

I looked at Roddy. He didn't say anything. I had a lot of questions, but they weren't the sort to shout across the room.

"Do you want me to take you home now?" I asked instead.

He shook his head, left the doorway, and walked down the driveway. I ran to catch up.

"Roddy, it's going to take you forever to walk home. Let me drive you."

"It's fine. My dad is working on a site in town, and I'll catch a ride from there."

He kept walking, and I thought that was going to be the end of it, but then he turned around, looking at the sunglasses in his hand before he looked at me. He opened his mouth to say something. Then he closed it, shook his head, put on his sunglasses, and turned to leave.

He didn't step forward, but looked back at me over his right shoulder, his profile rigid.

"What's her name?"

No emotion and in any other context, innocuous. I started to answer, but my throat was dry. I coughed to clear the words.

"Virginia Stanley."

A slight nod and Roddy walked away.

CHAPTER 21: LU

The music was still playing when I went back into the shop, but low enough to blend with the noises from both sides of the windows. On the outside it was a typical day – birds chirping, tires rhythmically spinning on the road, the sigh of a screen door opening and closing, and the rumble of the garbage truck a few streets away. We needed to take the trash out.

The inside was a stopped space, the only movement coming from the music and fans. One packed box and so many empty ones told a story about work a long way from finished. Virginia knew what went where. I tiptoed around the obstacle course, making my way to the kitchen and basement stairs. Virginia was sitting on the bottom step. I sat next to her.

"That was awkward."

"I'm sorry."

"Don't apologize, and it's none of my business, but you and Roddy …"

I wasn't sure how to finish the question I'd started. Thankfully, Virginia nodded, and I didn't have to. Then a melodramatic thought took hold – a thought I wasn't going to ask, but my eyes got big about. Virginia looked and laughed. There were some tears mixed in, too, and I looked away, giving her space to let both run through.

"No, Lu," she said after a minute, "Roddy is not Danny's dad, but that would make a better story than the truth."

She looked at me, her eyes steady.

"Danny's dad could have been any number of men. I know it's not Roddy because the timing is off."

"Okay."

"'Okay'?" she asked, her tone carrying sarcasm I hadn't heard before. "No judgment?"

"It's not my business, other than I happened to be left in the middle of the room after you ran to the basement and Roddy ran home."

She started laughing again. "Is that what happened?"

"That's what it felt like."

"You'd think after we …"

Virginia left the sentence unfinished. She took a breath and shook her head.

"I met him in a bar one night. It was crowded by the time I got there, but for once I wasn't there to meet someone – a big step up for me. I sat next to him without noticing him, but as soon as I did, my plan sort of shot to hell."

She looked at me to see whether I was tracking.

"I am a red-blooded female," I confirmed.

"So you get it, even if you wouldn't do it," Virginia said.

"Why would you say that?"

"You don't seem like the one-night stand type."

"Does it count if it's your ex-boyfriend who you're living with, but not sleeping with, but then you sleep with him to see if you can live with him?"

"That's a confusing sentence," Virginia said.

"It was a confusing situation."

I held up the bag of books I'd brought in from the car.

"Maybe these can help."

I meant it as a joke, and I took out the one on top – *Gently Flows Her Heart*. Virginia's smile was like one reserved for an old friend.

"I've read this."

She looked at me, reading the disdain on my face.

"You don't like this book?"

I shook my head.

"Have you read it?"

Another no.

"Try it. The good people are good, and the bad people are bad. It's refreshing."

I handed over the other two and reserved Virginia's recommendation for my back pocket.

CHAPTER 22: JACKSON

Roddy came over with wings, a six pack, and a hypothetical – at least that's how he started the conversation on my back stoop. "Patio" is how the ad for the rental had put it, but the cement rectangle barely fit two folding chairs. We put the food on a five-gallon bucket I turned upside down on the grass.

"Say you sleep with someone, and you don't remember her name after – not that you would do that."

"I do know Kate's name," I said.

"One woman. That's so strange."

"About as strange as many."

"You're telling me you never think about …"

"I'm telling you I try to keep my mind and body on the same line. I'm not saying I'm perfect. Keep going with what you came here to talk about."

"That's it."

"That's not a full thought."

"I figured you'd sort out the rest, being a pastor, though I'm sure no one from the church has ever come to you with something like this."

I washed down the spice from my first chicken wing with some beer and threw the bone away. My fingers were covered in hot sauce, and I'd forgotten to bring out paper towels. I wiped them in the grass instead.

"There you go again," I said.

"What do you mean?"

"Thinking you're the worst person in the world. You have no idea what people come to me with. Now where did you see this person?"

"It was at Penny Thrift. Did you know Lu is re-opening the store?"

"I've heard people talking about it."

"She has a woman helping her."

"Who?"

"That was the same question I asked Lu after I saw her."

"Did you get her name?"

"Virginia Stanley."

A memory took shape. "She makes clothes out of old t-shirts. Lu wrote a story about her last year. That was a smart move, bringing her in to help with the shop," I continued. "If Louisa knows anything about sewing, she never talked about it with me."

I could keep going, but Roddy just sat there holding his beer. He normally paced two drinks to my one. I don't know how many, if any, of the words I'd said registered with him. I leaned forward.

"What happened?"

He put beer down, and leaned his head back against his hands, looking at the sky before turning to look at me.

"I'm not sure how long ago it happened – a couple years, maybe? But it was the same shit as always – my dad riding me like I'm the one running the business into the ground when he can barely remember his own name by the middle of the afternoon.

"That night I decided to do the same, and I wanted to go somewhere I didn't know anyone. There's a bar on the north side of town – another limestone building in a row of limestone buildings.

"I was one drink down when she walked in. Virginia doesn't look anything like Lu, but she has the same quality – trying so hard to go unnoticed that you notice."

I knew it exactly. "And?"

"She sat next to me at the bar, but she was surprised when I said hello. We didn't talk much after that. I don't think I noticed she was still sitting next to me until a couple hours later. At that point, we realized we could help each other out."

I shook my head. "That's one way to put it."

"I didn't want to offend your sensibilities before you preach tomorrow."

We were quiet for a while. For my part because I still wasn't sure what Roddy was looking for. We'd been here before with him touching down on what seemed like regret. The feeling usually passed as quickly as the words left his mouth.

"This threw me today, Jack. I don't know why. It's not even the worst."

"Sometimes the worst things we do aren't enough to throw people. There's not a formula for it."

Roddy nodded. Then he looked at me and said something I didn't expect.

"I've never wanted to be you. You're the best person I know. You make good choices, but I've never wanted your life."

I laughed.

"I've wanted to be you, though," I said.

There was no reason for him to believe me. I turned the beer in my hands, wondering how to follow up what I'd said. Roddy kept me in a category, and I did the same with him. It made the friendship manageable. Why would I let him in? I'd told myself he wouldn't understand, but the opposite was true. Roddy probably understood my struggles better than anyone.

I finished my beer, set the empty bottle next to his untouched one, and looked at him.

"There have been many times I've wanted to turn one of those into six and get out of town on Friday without coming back Sunday," I said. "And I get what happened at the bar, but I wouldn't call it 'helping each other out.' It's want – plain and simple."

A moment replayed of Louisa and I on her parents' deck. We'd gotten pizza to eat at her house with Gracie and Ted. When they left, I realized I'd been waiting for them to go.

Roddy and I had switched sides, with me lost somewhere in the past and him leaning in, his elbows on his knees. He offered me his beer, and I shook my head.

"I don't understand why you act like what happened with Lu is a done deal," he said.

"You think I'm stupid."

"I'm not saying that."

"Sure you are."

He sat back, reclaiming his beer and downing half of it while I grabbed another chicken wing. "Okay, I am. I think you're being stupid. And I think you're doing the same thing you did with Kate. If you're going to insist on being with one woman, don't you think it should be the right one?"

"I've been down this road with Louisa, and it didn't end well."

"She came back changed," he noted.

"How do you know?"

"She told me, in the way she gets around to telling people about things."

I nodded. "She's a loner, that won't change for her, and if you're one of ones she lets in - man. There's something special about that. She's not for me, though. Look at what I do. Look at my life. I tried throwing away being a pastor when I threw away everything else, and here I am. Set aside the idea of one woman or many. If I'm going to be with anyone, she needs to be in this life with me. Can you see that?"

After a few seconds Roddy nodded. "Much as it pains me."

"There's a place you can take those thoughts of yours," I reminded him, ready to close the self-revelatory part of this conversation.

"How so?"

I rolled my eyes. "How about an apology to Virginia Stanley?"

"I'm going to let it go."

CHAPTER 23: LU

Virginia and I ended Saturday with the upstairs of Penny Thrift packed and a plan to move the boxes the next day. The idea required an empty basement, and Penny Thrift's was full.

There's a fine line between hoarding and thrifting. Grandma wasn't an acquirer, thanks to her thrifty side, but that same side stopped her from throwing away anything. Add a quilting business to all of this, and we had the basement of Penny Thrift: a tidy but packed space, half-filled with floor-to-ceiling shelves covered in folded fabric. The other half of the basement was divided between a fabric prep area with an industrial-sized washer and dryer, an ironing board that hinged down from the wall and an iron I'd never been able to maneuver without using both hands. Across from that was the shipping center with a large square table to hold a computer and piles of shipping supplies. File cabinets lined the wall behind the stairs. I opened one that Sunday and pulled out a warranty for two washing machines ago that expired in 1981.

I turned to Virginia, who'd met me here after church with Danny.

"I vote for throwing it all out," I said.

"No!"

"Why not? This fabric wasn't good enough to be upstairs in the first place."

"You don't know that."

"You don't know if it's worth sorting to find out."

"Yes, I do. Take the orange fabric for the rooster napkins you asked me to make for your grandma. I had to search an hour to find it, and Danny was screaming for lunch."

It sounded a bit too fantastical. I stuck with the facts in my rebuttal.

"I've never heard Danny scream."

Virginia shifted him to her other hip and plucked the bagel he'd been munching on straight out of his mouth. In two seconds, his scream saturated the basement. I covered my ears. Virginia gave the bagel back to Danny.

"I got the lady to sell me the orange t-shirt for a quarter," she said.

"So, you're telling me you want us to sort through all this based on the one time you took an hour to find an orange t-shirt for 25 cents to make rooster napkins?"

"Not all orange is orange, Lu."

I felt like I'd enrolled in a strange philosophy class. I took a good look at the teacher, who'd bound her hair in a messy bun with a tie-dyed bandana designed from dozens of fabrics she'd stitched together from t-shirt scraps. Her black t-shirt was understated, but still deconstructed and reconstructed to fit her perfectly.

I also sported a post-church bun, t-shirt, and jeans – the casual, looser, and nondescript cousin to her outfit. It did nothing for me.

"All of this is free," Virginia said. "We just have to go through it."

I raised my hands in surrender.

"You are like Grandma, and this is going to take all day."

"It will take more than one day."

I called my family to help and assigned everyone a station. Virginia took fabric. I set up stools for Nana and Mom by the file cabinets. The nieces had Danny, who now that he had three cute girls to look after him turned into a different version of Danny. Dad helped Ted demo the first floor.

For Gracie, I had a chair at the shipping table in the basement.

"It's important you not move from here."

She rolled her eyes but sat.

"I need your help with something," I said.

"Is this because you feel sorry for me?"

I lied. "No. Can you keep a secret from Ted?"

She lied. "Yes."

"I have no clue what to do with the upstairs of this place. I want it to be a shop, but not just a fabric shop. I want it to be more than a shop."

"Why?"

"Well, I'll be working here, and it's not like I have a dream of working in retail. Also, it'd be nice to have an inventory I could talk about. Do you have any ideas?"

"Nope, but I know where to go."

She swiveled around to the computer and pulled up Instagram.

I made like a project manager for the most of the afternoon – a flashy title for asking people if they needed help and being told mostly no. The times I was told yes resulted in a trip up or down the stairs. I think Ted was making stuff up toward the end to test my compliance and endurance, but I didn't care. Each square foot of empty space in the basement meant more space for the boxes from the first floor, which meant renovation, and then …. something … and we'd open! I'd worry about the something later. Right now, I was content in the clearing.

So, I didn't complain when Roddy showed up.

I followed Virginia's eyes to Roddy's and his eyes from her to Danny. I saw him figuring.

"You have a kid?" he asked.

"You smell like a pond," she said.

I laughed, and both looked at me like this wasn't funny.

"Oh, come on," I said. "Don't you think after you … and you … and this is the first time you've talked since …"

Now they looked at me like I was the crazy lady. I looked at Gracie, who looked interested. She didn't know the half of it.

Later, I mouthed to her.

Ted came down the stairs, and I asked Roddy and him to move the file cabinets we'd emptied to the detached garage – assuming there was room – and move the last of the boxes downstairs. Virginia finished the shelf she was working on and left with Danny. I walked over to Gracie.

I'm not much of a social media person. I'd used it for work, but I didn't have a personal account. I'd looked at Penny Thrift's feed once since I'd learned I inherited the shop, but what I saw – sale ads and inventory pictures – didn't hold my attention. From what I remember, the followers looked like a list of customers Grandma had followed back.

Gracie started with the list and added about 200 people over the afternoon. Some had followed us back, and the account names interested me. I pointed to one about a flower farm.

Gracie clicked, opening a world of flower fields and bouquets. I wanted to step into each picture.

"I want all of those."

"You should tell her when you see her."

"What do you mean?"

Gracie clicked over to a spreadsheet where she'd listed everyone she'd followed in increasing order according to their mileage from Dunlap's Creek. Flower Lady, Katie Lee, was number five and ten miles away.

"She brings her flower bar to the Farmer's Market on Saturdays. Did you ever run into her when you helped Grandma Pat sell pierogies last summer?"

"What's a flower bar?"

Gracie clicked a picture of flowers organized by stems in separate buckets that women circulated to build their own bouquets. It looked doable and fun. I wanted Penny Thrift to be more than fabric, but how could I use the space to host something like this and for it to still make sense? Gracie saw the question on my face.

"It's a 'something,'" she answered. "I don't think you have anything to lose by calling up or visiting a few of these places. You'll at least come away with some tips for running a business around here, which is more than either of us knows anything about."

"We're done!" Ted shouted as he came downstairs to help Gracie up the stairs. I took her seat and kept scrolling, liking the profile thumbnails of every person she had followed and not knowing what to do with any of it.

Roddy came down the stairs and walked to the computer.

"What's that?"

"A third option," I murmured, clicking over to a fiber artist who did contemporary embroidery wall hangings.

"It looks like what Virginia does. Are you going to invite me over to dinner for helping out?"

"Sure, though you do smell like a pond. What were you doing before you came here?"

"Fishing with Jack."

I looked over his shoulder at where the file cabinets had been and saw a crawl space in the upper half of the wall, hidden until now and empty, except for one box with faded illustrations of mason jars on the side. I walked over. The impressions of the jars were still molded into the cardboard, and I half expected to see rows of them when I opened it but lying on the top were fabric scraps that matched the hexagons from the quilt behind the register. I smiled, wondering whether it bothered Grandma that she hadn't used them all.

Emptying the box on my bed was like a game of Clue in trying to guess its significance to Grandma. The fabric scraps were easy. I assumed the old photographs were family members, but I didn't know their names. There was a pack of cigarettes built to last. I turned one over in my hand, recalling the smoking habit Grandma kicked after I finished sucking my thumb in the first grade. That was the promise, and I'd never seen her smoke again. Maybe these were for emergencies. There were a couple of thimbles, other sewing items I couldn't name, a recipe for strawberry preserves, and two tarnished silver candlesticks. At the bottom sat a small stack – an address book, a couple sewing patterns, and a notebook.

I opened it, predicting measurements, recipes, grocery lists or any of the other notations I'd seen her jot down. Grandma was more the doing than the pondering type. It's strange she'd keep a journal, and a quick flip of the dates from front to back showed she hadn't kept it for long. The entries spanned a year, with none longer than a paragraph. Why bother?

The first entry answered my question:

I woke up in a ditch yesterday and saw Jesus. He was holding out his hand to me. I went to church this morning to ask the pastor if seeing this made me crazy. He said it made me saved if I believed what it meant. Since I was at church and not in the ditch, I guessed that had to count for something. I told him I planned to come back next Sunday. He said to write down what happened in the meantime so I wouldn't forget. How could I forget seeing Jesus in a ditch? He said I'd be surprised what people forget. So, I'm writing it down.

I turned the pages – too quickly for a small journal and the only one of its kind. *Slow down*, I told myself, but I read as fast as I could, and I never wanted it to end. Until I did.

CHAPTER 24: LU

Anyone witnessing my scramble through the church history piles in my basement workroom on Monday morning would have sensed a woman renewed in her work. I was opening stuff, I was closing stuff, I was making new piles, and pushing aside those piles to look for more stuff.

They told me the Bible study was full. They said the deadline had passed for the cookbook entries this year. I could drop off Mark, but they didn't need my help with the kids on Sundays.

The awe I'd felt over the first pages of Grandma's journal had turned still. In the end, I was glad the notebook was small. I wondered whether she felt the same in writing the last entry as I felt in reading it.

I'm going to stick it out, but I don't know why. We go to church for the same Jesus, but who I am is not who they are, and they aren't like the Jesus who held out his hand to me in the ditch. I think they would have left me there.

Her journal was of a woman stopped in every step forward, and it didn't sync with what I knew. My family was a church family. It was a huge part of my life and formed the core of my distaste as I grew up. A girl can take only so much church, I posited, but no one in my family felt the same way, Grandma in particular. She was always doing stuff for the church. She enjoyed both the work and the people. If she hadn't, she would have said so and stopped. That's how she operated.

I sat back on my heels, remembering the week she died. All I saw were people – people coming through our house with enough food to start a co-op and people filling every square-inch, sitting and standing, at her funeral. If I hadn't been family and granted a choice spot at the burial, I wouldn't have seen the grave through the crowd. In her will she'd given her stuff away to specific people, every item with a name.

I had no idea what happened between year one and year now, and I still didn't know much about year one after reading the journal. Grandma wrote her paragraphs sparse and objective. She never mentioned names. I searched the piles for more, but everything was vanilla and without clues. Grandma had recorded the cookbook incident about a month into her journal. I found the cookbook from that year. It was one of the ones she wasn't in. I also found the corresponding meeting minutes for when they planned it, but all it contained was the basics: the date, a list of who was present, what was discussed, and action items.

Grandma's journal showed another side — a story about who wasn't on that list and unrecorded conversations. This was not the story the church had commissioned me to write, but it was the only story I could now see.

CHAPTER 25: LU

Virginia asked if she could hold her Bible study at Penny Thrift later that week, and my first reaction was a pass. This week had gone like last week, with me observing various church happenings and interviewing people except I was now on the lookout for a meta-narrative I wasn't finding and making zero progress on what I was supposed to be doing.

Why did Grandma save that stinking journal? Why did I read it? I had no answers, still Virginia was looking at me for an answer about her Bible study. A good Christian girl wouldn't say no. An angsty one shouldn't either.

"It's messy," I said instead.

"So are the people in my Bible study," she said.

"Okay," I agreed, albeit reluctantly.

Penny Thrift was messy. When we left on Sunday, the carpet had been removed and the tack strips were up. Since we were moving Penny Thrift away from being only a quilt shop, Dad and Ted had taken the shelves down, leaving a rectangular space that felt too wide. I mentioned it at dinner on Sunday, and Gracie pulled up the Pinterest boards she'd made. One board was for store interiors. Light and open, the pictures were inviting. I loved Penny Thrift, but it was hard for me to see how it could look like anything other than a ranch house converted to a store.

Ted started sketching. By the time I'd gone upstairs for my ill-fated snoop into Grandma's memory box, he'd diagrammed a glass and iron partition to create two spaces that kept the sense of one. Embedded was a sliding door to form a separate room for more of the 'something' I was still figuring out.

By Thursday, tools were everywhere, and right now, Dad was measuring and cutting planks to replace some of the rotted ones in the hardwood floor. Sawdust permeated, and I loved the smell – sweet, deep, and the perfect pairing to the apple I munched on as I watched Dad work at a slow pace that disregarded his deadline. Virginia's group would be here at the end of the hour.

I loved watching Dad work. He was patient and confident. He approached his work like an art, often taking steps back as if to catch a vision before digging into the next step. Listening to the sound of the saw and hammer felt like quiet. I was more content than I'd been all week.

"Do you always know what you're doing?" I asked him as he marked a board with a pencil before standing to carry it the saw.

"I know the order of things. You have to measure before you cut, but that doesn't mean either goes according to plan."

"What do you do when they don't?"

"I figure it out."

"And when that doesn't work?"

"I take a break."

"And when that doesn't work?

"I let it go and work around it, best as I can. I've never done a flawless project, but I keep getting asked to do more work. I don't think perfection is the point."

He was about to make a cut, but he pulled up his safety goggles and turned to me.

"Something on your mind, kiddo?"

I'd thought about asking him about Grandma all week, but he was young at the time of her ditch. His information would be secondhand, if he knew about it at all.

Virginia came in through the back door, ending the need to respond. The three of us righted the space – Dad moving tools next to the walls, Virginia setting up refreshments in the kitchen, and me doing a quick sweep before I set up folding chairs I borrowed from the church.

Dad left, and Virginia shifted the chairs from my oblong circle into a round one.

"Are you one of those people who re-loads your dishwasher after someone else has loaded it for you?" I asked.

"You're assuming someone has done that for me before," she said.

When Grandma first gave me the skirt from Virginia, she'd mentioned Danny's father wasn't around. The more I got to know her, I was starting to sense no one was around or maybe never had been. But every time Virginia said something like this, it was with the tone of a closed door. I could ask a follow-up question, but I didn't think she'd answer it.

"How did you meet my grandma?" I asked instead.

"I lived in Dunlap's Creek my whole life, so who knows how many times we had seen each other? But we met on Etsy. The job I was working had cut my hours. Up until then, I sewed for myself. I never thought anyone else would want it, but I grabbed a couple shirts and skirts from my closet and posted pictures on Etsy. Nothing sold at first, and I felt stupid for trying. I was ready to take my page down when your grandma messaged me. She asked me to meet her here. When she saw my clothes up close, she said I had a talent. No one ever told me that. About anything. She offered to host a trunk show, and I needed to make rent."

"Did you?"

"Barely. Plus, I had to sell half of my closet to do it. Then you posted the picture of the skirt on Instagram and wrote the article in the paper. Suddenly, I had orders and a wait list."

Virginia paused in her reorganization of the food and drinks she'd laid out in the kitchen. She looked at me.

"I never thanked you."

I wanted to respond and say it was nothing, but what she'd shared felt like too much to form words around, let alone swallow.

Thankfully, Virginia changed the topic.

"So, this group tonight was something your grandma started. I think whenever she offered to help someone, like she did with me, she'd invite them to this. A lot of women would come once out of obligation, but a small group of us has stuck with it. Most of us never went to church, and a lot of us still don't go. What happens here is pretty simple. We take a book of the Bible a couple verses at a time and try to make sense of it."

One knock and one woman came, and ten minutes later there were six — none of whom I knew.

Virginia introduced me and explained why the store was a mess. The group had met here once a week while the store was open, but in the last four months assumed a gypsy rotation that didn't work for anyone because they all lived in small apartments or with other people.

It's funny how you can go from dread to gratitude in a moment, but that's what happened as I watched the women sit, open their Bibles, and start talking. I wasn't invited to join, but Virginia didn't seem to expect I would leave, either. There was too much work to do in the store.

I stuck around and did what I was supposed to do when I'd been watching Dad. First, stain swatches for the floor. I opened the cans as quietly as I could and rubbed the stains on the scrap planks with an old t-shirt, like Ted had shown me. Then, I moved to the walls. Gracie had chosen ten variations of gray from almost white to charcoal. I painted the samples in a slow succession along the wall, eavesdropping as I went.

The group had started the book of Ephesians, and I was struck again by how all my churching growing up had churched my brain without me realizing it. I knew a lot of Bible. With Jackson's sermons, I knew the high and lowlights of Abraham's story. I was still figuring out what they meant, but it was nice to work with facts I could recall, even if from a fuzzy place.

It was the same with this group. I knew "epistle" meant "letter," and Ephesians was a letter written by Paul. I knew Paul's story — from a Jew who had persecuted Christians to an apostle for Christians. I knew what apostle meant, and I knew Paul spent the rest of his life telling non-Jews about Jesus. I knew the missionary journeys he took and could still draw them with a crayon, courtesy of my time in Sunday school. I might still be able to find Ephesus on a map.

These women didn't have the benefit of my church upbringing, and they didn't carry the baggage. The last time I'd been in a Bible study was high school youth group, and we were concerned with parroting the right answers. These women were more interested in asking questions.

"Who is Paul again and why do we care what he says?"

"He wrote the thing."

"He calls himself an 'apostle.' Is that some sort of job title?"

"And he keeps talking about the 'will of God.' Is that what God wants? What happens if what God wants isn't what I want?"

"This might not apply to us. He says he's writing to saints. He can't mean real people, right?"

"Why does Paul name-drop Jesus three times in one sentence?"

"What does grace mean? What does peace mean? Are these different or does Paul just like to hear himself talk?"

"He's definitely a talker."

On and on they went, and it was interesting to hear them explore answers. Each woman came prepared to discuss but went about it in a different way, with some relying on footnotes from their Bibles while others had listened to sermons online. Virginia was a skillful facilitator. She collected what women shared and shuffled it around like she did with her fabrics until a design took shape. She pitched this back to the group to see what they made of it. The conversation was honest and friendly and earnest. These first verses could be thrown away as an inconsequential salutation, but the group treated them like an important start.

"I like the third one," one of the women noted as they packed up to leave. She was talking about the sample on the wall. Her name was Sarah, and she was the one who'd anchored the definition of grace in "more."

"But only if she chooses the last stain. If she goes lighter on the floor, then she'll need to go darker on the wall," another woman said, whose name I couldn't remember.

The rest of the group clustered after they folded their chairs, offering an array of opinions I tracked in a diagram on the wall itself. I'd take a picture tomorrow and send it to Gracie.

They left with a plan to read the next few verses of Ephesians, rewrite the verses they'd unpacked, and answer questions as if they were writing a letter. How would you label yourself? Who would you write to? What would be the first thing you would want someone to know?

CHAPTER 26: LU

Friday was a field trip to the flower farm, and I took Nana Bea with me. She'd been in charge of the town's garden club since the dawn of time and could talk shop better with the owner, Emily Lockwood, than me. She also had a working knowledge of Grandma Pat.

"What was your impression of Grandma Pat when you first met her?" I asked as soon as we backed out of her driveway in the Caddy, her preferred mode of transport.

"She wore too many colors for a woman with red hair."

I waited for more.

"And ..." I prompted.

"There's no 'and' – that's what I thought. Your mother had been dating your father all summer. We never thought it'd go beyond a summer romance. Then she came to us in the fall with the hare-brained idea of marrying him. I asked Mark and Pat to dinner as a stalling technique. Your father was fine. Polite and quiet, though I worried about how he'd provide for Mary since he didn't come from much and wasn't planning to go to college. But Pat ..."

I turned my head and caught a smile at the edge of her lips.

"Pat was wearing an over-sized sweater that kept slipping off her shoulder. After a while, I realized she intended for the outfit to look like that. The length of her skirt was respectable enough, ending a few inches above her ankles, but it looked like a quilt. None of the colors matched the yellow in her sweater, by the way."

I could see it – Grandma sticking out like a fashionable ragamuffin in Nana's muted parlor where the fabrics came in chintz or velvet.

"What else?"

"She was loud, but I don't need to tell you that."

I nodded and beckoned with my hand for more. Nana seemed stumped.

"That's all," she said.

"That can't be all."

"It was for me, for a while anyway. Our paths didn't cross much until after your grandfather died. We weren't in the same circles."

Between Dunlap's Creek and anywhere are corn and soybean farms. I'd never been to a flower farm before, and I didn't know what to expect when I turned left onto the long, gravel drive about ten minutes out of town. On either side was a manicured lawn leading up to typical farmhouse with white siding, black shutters, and a large porch with a swing.

The back of the property looked like nothing I'd ever seen. There were fields of flowers planted in tidy rows, plus a couple hoop houses. Emily handed us each a pair of scissors and encouraged us to build our own bouquets during the tour. Nana had dressed down for the occasion, as if in anticipation of this offer. She rarely wore pants or anything less than a two-inch pump, one detail she and Grandma Pat had in common, but today she wore chinos, white sneakers and her periwinkle blue sweater set. She secured her wide-brimmed straw hat with the drawstring under the chin.

I dove into cutting right from the first row, not listening to any of the details about the common or Latin names of the flower varieties because I knew I wouldn't remember them. They triggered questions from Nana, though, about things like soil pH and sun patterns. She pointed to one bush I'd cut a stem from, questioning how Emily cultivated it to grow large blooms in a south-facing location when east-facing was recommended. Emily had a ready answer, and I marveled at Nana's inner compass rose. Why did she have me drive her everywhere when she could pinpoint direction against the sun's location at any given time of day? I'd be lost without my GPS.

I clipped a bloom from every row, give or take. Emily paused long enough in her exposition to see my armful of mish-mash and took us straight to her "cut-hut" – a large shed, outfitted with its own mini-porch. The inside was rimmed with galvanized trashcans, the labels on their lids identifying the soil, compost, or fertilizer they contained. Above these were shelves holding vases, burlap, ribbons, and other odds and ends people could use to make their bouquets. A sturdy metal table spray-painted in a light blue paint, more chipped than covered, occupied the center of the space.

Nana's bouquet was a mix of peonies and lilies. It didn't need anything other than a ribbon to secure it. She chose one in light pink satin and secured it with two pins. I didn't pretend to know what I was doing, but handed my flowers to Emily, who spread them on the table. The best way to organize variety was by color, she said. In less than ten minutes, I had three bouquets, each placed in a tin coffee can.

Emily took us to her patio and brought out fresh lemonade, garnished with mint she plucked from a waist-high wooden box to the left of the patio door.

"That's a good way to grow mint," Nana said.

"It still spreads to the lawn, and I have to root it out a few times a year," Emily said, "but I drink my morning coffee out here, and the smell wakes me up."

I inhaled. The only mint I'd considered to this point was the gum kind. One sip of the lemonade confirmed its magical powers.

"How did you start all of this?" I asked, way more curious about the back-story behind the place than its flora field guide.

"With these herb boxes along the patio."

Emily wasn't from here, but her husband, Martin, was. They moved back when his mom's health failed, and she couldn't live on her own anymore. The timing was good. Both had retired from their community college teaching jobs: him in engineering and her in botany.

"We were planning to move anyway, but to a condo on a golf course. That was five years ago, but I can't imagine why we ever thought we'd be happy doing that.

"Taking care of Tom's mom in those first few years was tough, and our golf game tanked fast because we felt bad about leaving the other one alone with his mom for long periods of time. To cut down on the stress, we spent as much time as we could outside around here instead. Tom built these herb boxes for me with wood he found in the barn. Then we tilled the area to the right of patio for a kitchen garden. I started planting flowers around the border as an attempt to keep the pests away, but I kept cutting them to make bouquets. I liked bringing the outside in for Tom's mom. I planted a second bed that fall, for flowers this time, and from there I became sort of obsessed."

I held my hand to my forehead to shade my eyes from the bright sun as I surveyed her flower spread, wondering if what I could see was all there was.

"There are worse obsessions," I said.

She planted three more flower beds the next spring, and Tom built the hoop house so she could work with seeds through the winter. It wasn't until the following year Emily determined what to do with all of the flowers. She started with flower shares for people to pick up once a week during the growing season. This was the first year she rented a stall at the Farmer's Market. Her next move was to break into the bridal market, but she didn't know where to start.

I told her about Dunlap's Creek wedding market, a funny way to put it, but it was true. A lot of people got married here. I shared recommendations for vendors from the Creek Wedding Fest I'd organized last year, and I promised to email her their contact information later.

"Would you be willing to come to Penny Thrift's store opening?" I blurted, my lips forming the words before my brain could catch them.

"Sure. Send me the date. I'll bring a couple people who will make great customers."

"Thank you, but I meant as a vendor."

"Isn't Penny Thrift a fabric shop?"

This is where improv kicked in, something I'm horrible at. I credited the sugar from the lemonade for helping me make a go of it.

"We aren't reopening it as just a fabric store, but more as a place to draw women together. We had an artisan alley of small businesses at Fest last year, and they had the most foot traffic of anyone. It's not that people around here don't want to buy local, it's that they don't always know where to find it, especially the people who haven't built a buzz yet. Penny Thrift will make a good starting place for businesses and buyers, and we're redesigning the space for women to do more than shop. There's going to be a separate room in the main area where you could hold a DIY flower bouquet class, for example.

It came in a rush. If Emily missed any of what I'd said, I wouldn't have had the wherewithal to repeat it. I held my breath, but her eyes matched her smile.

"Sign me up."

We finished our tour, with Nana and Emily resuming their flower talk like I hadn't given the pitch of my life. I kept to the back and didn't take my flower scissors along this time. I was so distracted, I'd probably snip off a finger. Nana cut some roses from one of the hoop houses for another small bouquet, and when she mentioned she'd never grown flowers from seed before, Emily gave her a small flat of annuals. We loaded it all in the car. I kept my cool as I said goodbye, turned the car around in the driveway, waved, and drove away at a responsible speed.

Once I reached the road, I put the Caddy in park and stomped my feet in a drumroll. Nana kept her hands folded in her lap.

"So, you're holding an opening?" she asked after I'd finished whooping.

"I think I got a little carried away."

"It's a good idea. Everyone loves a party."

Except me. I didn't know what I was getting into, but I also needed to set a deadline to open Penny Thrift if I was ever going to do it.

I collected my hair into a ponytail and readjusted my clothes, twisted a bit by my happy dance. It was a beautiful morning and Nana was still wearing her hat. I was pretty sure she'd let me roll down the windows for the drive home, but I looked at her to make sure. She nodded, and then she said, "You're going to need help."

Yes, especially since up until 10 minutes ago, I thought I'd re-open after I finished the church project.

"I'm going to need help."

She smiled and looked to her left, checking for cars before I turned right for home.

"I will help you."

CHAPTER 27: JACKSON

I never knew what I'd find when I visited Rebecca's class, especially at the end of the school year.

"Crowd control with a learning bonus" was how she'd described it, but I thought Rebecca was selling herself short. When I slipped into her class Friday, the kids seemed focused, divided into small groups to practice lines and make costumes out of oversized t-shirts. One group was drawing a backdrop on the white board. When Rebecca saw me, she enlisted my help to move desks for the upcoming performance.

It was Romeo & Juliet, the 30-minute fifth grade version. Before getting her Master's in teaching, Rebecca had double-majored in theater and literature. She'd written her senior thesis on one of Shakespeare's plays. I could never remember which one because I don't like Shakespeare, which I'd confessed to her on our third date after pretending to be interested on dates one and two.

She wasn't put off.

"You don't like Shakespeare because you don't understand Shakespeare."

"Who does? I know Latin and Greek, and I still don't get it."

"Yeah, but Shakespeare was English."

Then she stood up from the bench and recited something, like it was an audition. It was one of the first warm, weekend days of spring, and there were a lot of people walking on the path in the park. Those within hearing distance stopped and smiled. To my left, I saw someone taking a video on their phone. Then I gave Rebecca my full attention, still having no idea what she was saying. She said it well, though, and I clapped when she finished.

"Did you really stand up in the middle of the park and recite ...?"

"Sonnet 18," she finished for me. "Is that uncomfortable for you?"

"It will take more than that."
She grabbed my hand and pulled me to my feet.
"Repeat after me: 'Shall I compare thee to a summer's day?'"
"Shall I compare thee to a summer's day?"
"'Thou art more lovely and more temperate.'"
"'Thou art more lovely and more temperate," I said.
Rebecca smiled. "Why, thank you."
"You're welcome, but what did I say?"
"You don't know?"
"People don't talk like that."
"Maybe not now."
"I don't think they did back then, either."
She put her hands on her hips. "Are you going to ruin this for me?"
"No, ma'am."
"Okay, so now you say, 'Rough winds do shake …'"
"You're wonderful."
I'd been thinking it for a while — the joy, the ease Rebecca brought everywhere she went. She looked at me, tilting her head to the left.
"Are you trying to distract me, Jackson?"
I stepped closer. That's when I kissed her for the first time.
"That part doesn't happen until after the sonnet," she said.
"Should I take it back?"
Then she kissed me.

I assumed there would be none of that in today's performance and sure enough, every time a scene led up to a kiss, the chorus of students in the wings and the audience would fake vomit, making for some of the best acting of the day.

I should have seen it coming, but Rebecca had primed the class to rope me into playing the part of Friar Lawrence, who it turns out was a man with good intentions. But as the play went on, I started to wonder whether his meddling was the reason Romeo and Juliet died. He was the one who married the two with a hope of uniting the families. When that didn't work he settled on a re-uniting plan that involved a sleeping potion to make Juliet look dead. No one told Romeo, and he killed himself before she woke up. It was horrible stuff. The kid playing Romeo sat back up from his death scene to ask a question.

"Do pastors give people sleeping potions, Pastor Jackson?"

"Friar Lawrence was more of a priest," I explained, not sure where I was going with that.

"Have you ever married anyone in secret?"

"No."

"Helped someone get out of town?"

"No."

"What do you do all day?"

I shot a look to Rebecca, who was too busy laughing to help me out. I thought back through my week, trying to think of something to interest these kids, but came away half-bored myself.

"I study, and I meet with people."

The boy made a face – the face he should have made when he drank the poison in his death scene – and lay back down. Then it was Juliet's turn to die, which in the real play I remembered as being a quiet, contemplative moment, but the class turned it into a group effort, with each kid taking a turn to fall flat and show the rest how to do it right. The bell sounded, resurrecting them all, and they were off.

I had the room put back by the time Rebecca was done with bus duty.

"How come you never visit me at work?" I asked.

"You don't sell it well. Maybe if you'd said, 'meeting with people and talking in Latin or Greek,' I'd be more interested."

"I only know how to read in those, not make conversation."

"Looks like Shakespeare is more practical than your job skills."

"Practical?"

"It took one sonnet to get you to kiss me."

I laughed, pulling her to me. "So how come you don't speak to me in Shakespeare anymore?"

She put her hand on my jaw and whispered, "'O, here will I set up my everlasting rest, and shake the yoke of inauspicious stars from this world-wearied flesh. Eyes, look your last! Arms, take your last embrace; and, lips, O you the doors of breath, seal with a righteous kiss a dateless bargain to engrossing death!'"

"I don't think that's from a love scene."

She took a "Keep Up the Good Work!" sticker from her desk and put it on my chest.

Dinner that night was at my parents'. Dad and Mom waited for us at the door like they always did when they knew I was coming. If I ever came by without telling them first, they'd apologize they weren't at the door to greet me. Sometimes I wondered what would happen if I was late. How long would they stand there waiting?

Dad and Mom had the type of manners that were normal to me growing up, but rare in most places I'd been since. A lot of it had to do with what they'd carried from their conservative upbringing in small country churches where the only music they listened to was hymns on Sundays. There'd been no dancing at their wedding. They never called anyone by his or her first name until the person gave them permission. I don't think anyone from our church had ever gone to the hospital without Dad visiting and Mom making a meal.

Their generation also played a part. They were older than my friends' parents. Mom didn't have my sister until she was thirty, and I was her surprise ten years later. It wasn't a sheltered upbringing so much as maybe they'd raised us for a world that didn't exist outside their home. They'd moved here when they first married and never moved out. They kept everything they'd been given, even the repeats, like the "As for me and my house" from Joshua 24:15 embroidered and on display in four different rooms. That's a lot for a three bedroom ranch.

It only felt strange to me growing up when I'd bring friends over. Their houses had finished basements with TVs and video games we'd binge on all night because there wasn't a lights-out policy. We saw their parents when they'd replenish the pizza, chips, soda, and other packaged food my parents never had. In my friends' eyes, I could see how different – and strange – coming to my house was because it was always a sit-down dinner. There wasn't much to do inside, and one of my parents was always around to supervise, so we'd hang out in the backyard.

The only friend who ever really fit in was Roddy. Our home would have felt strange to him, but he never commented, which was his sign of appreciation. It was a family. My parents were here, and they cared about what we were up to – all the things he didn't have.

Bringing Rebecca here still felt like something new to a place that never changed. She could make herself fit anywhere – fill it up or break it up as necessary. Tonight, the stillness never had a chance. She was waving as she got out of the car and holding a conversation with my parents before she was up the walkway, recounting the events from the afternoon.

"I think Jackson has a career in acting if being a pastor doesn't work out," she concluded before she gave Mom a hug, and she and Mom went inside.

"Thinking about a career change, son?" Dad asked, also giving me a quick hug before sitting in one of the folding aluminum chairs better suited to a church picnic than the centerpiece of their front porch.

"Maybe." I sat next to him, ready to share what was on my mind. "I got a letter from my old church last week. You remember Pete, my assistant pastor? He'd been serving as interim since I left. I guess they finally selected a new guy, and this was the welcome letter."

"What are your thoughts on that?"

I laughed. "I need to get off my old church's mailing list."

Dad looked at me, an invitation to continue if I wanted.

"There was a picture of his wife and their two kids. It will probably put the church at ease that he's figured out parts of his life I couldn't."

"What appears isn't always what is."

I nodded. "I know."

I leaned back in the chair, carefully. The synthetic straps holding the aluminum together were ready to give away, at which point Dad would rebuild the frame with duct tape. Every time I sat here, I thought about buying my parents new chairs, but I'd done things like that before, and I knew how it would go. They'd keep them in a box, and in the meantime, they'd learn about someone who had a greater need and give them away. After all, these chairs weren't broken, just breaking. There was time yet.

We were quiet for a while, the only sounds coming from Mom and Rebecca setting the table.

"It bothers me, Dad. It bothers me that it bothers me," I said, thinking through the words as I spoke them.

"This man would have been prepped. The elders would have told him what happened with me, and maybe he reacted as I would in the same situation – not asking for more details than necessary. Maybe he would say he understood, all while making promises to himself he wouldn't mess up like I did."

"You're going pretty far back, Jackson."

"The past is important, Dad."

"As it informs the present and what you do with it. You know this. Think about what you're preaching on Sundays – not Abraham, the former pagan from Ur, but Abraham, the patriarch of God's people. It's a story about who we are becoming and what we're stepping into, not where we come from or who we used to be."

He turned to me, his eyes steady.

"How long are you going to hold on to what God has let go? Isn't it time to move on?"

My nod came before my agreement, but Dad didn't see it. He was now looking across the yard, his arms on his knees and his hands folded.

"We never wrote a letter to the church when you came back – mostly because everyone knew you. It was an expedient decision, but maybe not a wise one."

"It's better you didn't."

"But it might have been better for you if we had. Maybe it would have helped you see this isn't the final step in your reverse from your last church and your divorce, but a step into something new."

He reached over to squeeze my hand before he stood.

"Take another minute. I'll go inside to help Mom and Rebecca finish getting dinner ready.

The screen door whistled closed, and I heard Dad's voice join the mix. I wanted to go in, but I needed to clear my mind of letters and pictures first.

Releasing is both an instance and a process. The letter reminded me that even though I released what happened, I was still hanging on. I was grateful to be here, but Dad was right. I hadn't received the appointment as a step forward so much as a bandage to finish healing, and that was interesting because I was content here. I'd been building a life, but without claiming I was doing it.

Even if I hadn't heard her setting the table, I knew Rebecca was helping my mom. I knew she was asking questions about her day. She would remember Mom's answers and follow-up with her the next time she saw her.

If I got a call right now to leave, it wouldn't faze her. Rebecca would stay for dinner and make plans with my parents for the next time. Then she would check to see if I'd eaten yet and offer to bring me something if I hadn't.

It'd been a long time since anyone cared about me like this. There was respect and trust, and I hadn't felt the emptiness until she'd filled it. Paint in her hair, Shakespeare in the park, good with my family, the church, and kids. If there was a letter with a picture, I could see us in it. We would be standing, side-by-side, smiling at whoever was taking it.

I stood up, looking across yard as Dad had. In my mind, Louisa was there. She was doubt for me. She was a question. With her, it'd be a different picture. I doubt I'd notice the camera at all. I'd be looking at her.

Rebecca's voice found its way from the back of the house to the porch, calling us to dinner. Our family dinners before her were comfortable, but quiet – not surprising for a family that held to the proverb of two ears to hear and one mouth to speak. Rebecca was good at both.

CHAPTER 28: LU

Now that I'd committed to an opening for Penny Thrift, it was time to hash out the rest – like what the day would look like, and beyond that, what form the shop would take. I was expecting pushback from my family, but they were relieved. They knew how my uncertainty can sometimes stall me, and they were happy to see momentum, even if it was toward a hazy goal. Ted, who'd been content to let the place sit while I was in New York, was impatient now that we were investing time and money. It was all gone, he reminded me, until we re-opened. Virginia was ready to earn a paycheck. I was equal parts excited and terrified to see whether we could earn anything.

Since we'd pulled off Fest, we decided to run opening day in a similar way, as a celebration of local artistry by pulling in makers from around the area. I set the date for three weeks out, and we got to work, settling into our roles from before. This was a smaller deal on every level. The construction wasn't finishing a church this time, but refinishing floors, painting walls, and installing the glass-iron partition on the main floor of a 1500 square-foot house.

"It won't take more than two weeks," Ted told me.

"Which means three," Dad said.

They made a bet, and I decided not to worry about it.

Virginia, Gracie, and I were in charge of everything else. Grandma had built a solid customer base over the last two decades. These people would be the most likely to come to the re-opening, and they were expecting fabric. We planned to dedicate most of the vendor space on opening day, as well as the retail space shop in this first year, to textiles with a thrifty bent.

Virginia's designs fell in this category. She'd kept busy with custom orders since the article last year and wanted to try ready-made items. For the opening, she planned to test two lines: one, a fashion line of t-shirts and headbands and two, a home line of napkins and aprons. She'd asked Ted to move Grandma's cutting table from the front room to the kitchen, and I could always find her there, cutting up t-shirts or stitching them back together.

In recent years, Grandma had outsourced most of the quilting. Virginia contacted those women to see who was still interested. She found a fiber artist on the other side of the state who knit garments from recycled yarn. There was also a woman who made natural dyes and a woman who fashioned buttons and other sewing notions from antique jewelry. I saw a new sort of Penny Thrift taking shape, an eclectic little world where women could find sewn items of all kinds, each a centerpiece in its inherent uniqueness, or the materials to create their own.

The mission of making something from nothing went beyond fabric, and we decided to use the partitioned space as a maker's market of pop-up shops and workshops for different crafts to bring women in for different maker experiences – basically "fest" but in shop form, all year long.

Over the last week, Gracie doubled the names on her spreadsheet. We set up filters for Gracie's list – in state and handmade from repurposed materials – but even with these parameters, we had to choose which vendors to bring in. By this point, I was convinced that every town in America had at least one woman running a cottage industry selling jewelry, candles, wall art, natural beauty products, and stationery. I could see how Penny Thrift would be a physical hub for it all, both as a store and a gathering space to build a community around what was now a solo making and shopping experience.

We divvied the work with me planning opening day, Gracie planning pop-up shops, and Mom planning workshops. Nana tracked it all, not on the shared spreadsheet I'd set up, but in a notebook with her silver ballpoint pen.

The only pushback I received in that first week was from Roddy when I told him about my plan not to charge the vendors for booths on opening day. He'd brought me take-out Chinese on his way back into town that Thursday, and the smell reminded me I'd skipped lunch. Now it was seven and here was Roddy with fried rice and wontons. I popped one in my mouth and shared the plan that sounded so reasonable in my mind.

It stopped his wonton halfway to his mouth.

"Are you a non-profit?" he asked.

"No," followed by a heaping spoonful of fried rice – so greasy and too much salt. I didn't mind.

"Then you charge for space."

"How can I do that? I've never done something like this before. It's a big gamble."

"What would have happened if you hadn't charged any of the vendors for Fest last year?"

"That was different."

"In your mind. You are still putting these people in front of more foot traffic than most of them experience on a normal business day, in addition to advertising them to your Grandma's email list. Exposure brings a value they should pay for."

"Even if I've never done something like this before?"

"You did Fest."

"I've never run a business before," I clarified. "I'm thankful anyone is showing up."

"Say "thank you" and set a rate."

He kept going while I chowed down, stealing a wonton from his box because eating it didn't seem as important to him as lecturing me.

"How are you so confident, Roddy?" I asked when he broke long enough for a bite.

"I have to be. I need to put food on the table."

We were leaning against the countertops in the kitchen, and I looked out the window above the sink to the gravel driveway where he'd parked his sports car.

"You mean pay for your car."

"Right, to bring the food to put on the table tonight."

"Countertop," I corrected.

Dad and Ted had taken the old kitchen table to the detached garage when they brought in the cutting table for Virginia. I wasn't confident in my ability to move aside her fabric piles and put them back in their original places without her knowing. It was also likely I'd spill soy sauce on them.

"What's going on here?" Roddy asked with a gesture to the table, so casual it landed the opposite of how he intended.

I smiled. "You know how I know you're in town?"

"I tell you."

"You come here."

"You're always here."

"I'm here nights. I work at the church during the day."

"And nights are when I'm free," Roddy said.

I looked behind his back. There was another bag of Chinese food.

"That's a lot of food for two people," I said. "Were you expecting someone else?"

Virginia walked in on cue through the back door. It was Bible study night, and she reacted the same way she always did when she saw Roddy. She looked through him to me.

I held up a carton. "Want some?"

"I ate." She turned to go to the main room.

"I like your stuff," Roddy said, gesturing to the table again, and the look she returned made me wish we'd had another minute before she came in. I wasn't the expert, but my description of her work would have helped Roddy farther along than "stuff."

She didn't bother to respond, and the sound of her setting up chairs ended our conversation for tonight. Roddy put the untouched bag of Chinese in the fridge. I followed him to his car.

"If you want to talk to her …"

He gave me a warning look, and I hesitated. Roddy had made himself available to me over the last few weeks to talk work, but in his personal life he was as closed off as anyone I'd ever met. He didn't talk about himself. Where he wouldn't go, he didn't want me to go. But Virginia was here. I was here. If Roddy was going to be here, this needed to be said.

"If you want to talk to her, you need to start further back."

He shook his head, looking at Virginia through the shop window one more time.

After I said goodbye to Roddy, I drove to pick up Gracie, and we returned to Penny Thrift 20 minutes later. Officially, we were here on business and could talk uninterrupted. Ted was coaching Caroline's softball team tonight, and my parents were watching the younger two. Unofficially, I wanted to see what Gracie made of Bible study. I knew if she was interested, she'd join, thus creating a bridge for me to do the same – maybe tonight, next week, or next year. It was the pattern I'd relied on to break into high school circles, and I didn't see why it should work differently now.

It took ten minutes for her to ditch me at the kitchen table. By the end of the hour, she was participating like she'd been a part of this study from the beginning and had done the homework in preparation for tonight's session.

She hadn't, but I had, sort of. Unlike the girls here, I hadn't written anything, but I thought about it, and I'd re-read the first two verses of Ephesians every day, marveling at how Paul claimed his faith. The simplicity – *Paul, an apostle of Christ Jesus by the will of God* – left no room for misinterpretation.

What would it be like to be so open with who you were and what you believed? I still hadn't told anyone other than Jackson, in part because I was looking for words. I was versed in expressing doubt and questions, but belief was so new. It needed a new vocabulary, and the ones from my church childhood didn't fit.

I'd moved Grandma's computer from the basement to minimize trips up and down the stairs, and I hadn't moved from behind the giant screen since Bible study started. I gave the appearance of typing away, but I wasn't working. No, right now the introduction to my letter would say something like, Lu, an Undercover Note-Taker.

The group was working through the next few sentences in Paul's letter, which were tricky to understand, but I had enough sentence structure training over the years to puzzle together what he meant. I had fun doing it, too.

Virginia's group was not feeling the same way.

"I have no idea what verse six means," one woman said.

"Does 'predestined' mean we don't have a choice?" another said.

"What comes next is also confusing – *in accordance with his pleasure and will to the praise of his glorious grace, which he has freely given us in the One he loves.*"

"It means we belong."

The words came out clear and loud and from me. The group went quiet, looking to me for more.

I shook my head.

"That's all I've got."

"But how did you get it?" Virginia asked, and Gracie beckoned her hand for me to come over and sit in the empty chair next to her. I made it to the doorway of the kitchen.

"It's a long sentence, so I broke it into parts. Then, I asked the same question you did about what it meant."

"Can you show us how you did that?" a woman I didn't know asked.

To my left was a mural of wildflowers my nieces drew on the wall when I'd brought them here after school this week. This reminded me that Gracie needed to choose a wall color before she left tonight, so Dad could paint before Ted refinished the floors. I snatched one of the pencils from Virginia's worktable and continued my nieces' good work by writing the full sentence on the wall above their flowers.

In love he predestined us to be adopted as his sons through Jesus Christ, in accordance with his pleasure and will — to the praise of his glorious grace, which he has freely given us in the One he loves.

"Paul's writing is confusing because he put a lot of thoughts together in one sentence. We have to identify the individual thoughts and phrases and rework them into language we understand."

I underlined the first — *In love* — and held out the pencil to the group. "Who wants to underline the next one?"

It took a few seconds, but a woman came forward to underline the next one. My nod and smile were enough to encourage a few more women to try.

Then, I divided the group into pairs and gave each a phrase to figure out. The women took it from there with the same honesty from last week, and this time, Virginia tracked it all on the wall, circling keywords, writing definitions, and drawing lines to connect the thoughts. I didn't contribute again. I didn't go back to the computer, either. I sat down in the circle and watched it all happen, thinking how Grandma would have thought this was the best use of a wall. She'd be mad I thought of it first.

I took a picture of the group by the wall, sorry their night's work would be painted over this weekend. I needed to get back to mine, and Virginia offered to take Gracie home so I could finish.

The document I'd pulled up to finalize my marketing plan for the next two weeks was interrupted by Roddy, take-out Chinese, and Virginia. Now the bottom half was filled with Bible study notes. Tomorrow was soon enough to double check the publicity dates I'd set. I closed up shop.

And it would be a shop, I thought, as I walked the perimeter to turn off the lights. By the start of next week, there would be a new stain on the floor and a new color on the walls. The partition would follow, and then we'd stock inventory. Virginia's sketches of the space covered the fridge, but I had a good imagination, too. I could describe how it would be, but I hoped I would always remember how it looked now, on the eve of it all.

I was at the wall farthest from the flower-scripture scene, ready to turn off the last light. The only words I could read through the shadows were the circled ones written in Virginia's scrawling calligraphy. Loved. Chosen. Adopted. Grace. Through & In the One God Loves. Jesus Christ.

Jackson had talked about the promises of God from Genesis 15-17 on Sunday – both their universal and personal qualities. I could hear his voice as I recalled the sermon.

In this passage, we learn He is a God who sees. He sees Abram – not from a distant, high place, but as a father sees a child. God sees the fear inside him, which is why he says, "Do not be afraid, Abram. I am your shield, your very great reward."

He is a God of compassion, and so He hears the doubts of an old, childless man and answers them with a promise. Abram will have a son from his body. His descendants will cover the earth like the stars cover the sky.

He is a God of patience and so he hears Abram's doubts again. He binds the words into a promise through a covenant – one that requires God, not Abram, to keep. This is good for Abram because he will soon bear a son from his body, but by his plan, not God's, through his maidservant instead of his wife.

God is a God of mercy and grace. He responds again with a covenant of the same promises, but with more details this time. God renames whom he redeems, and he changes Abram's name to Abraham. In return, Abraham must be circumcised – a physical sign of who he belongs to.

Loved, chosen, adopted, grace, through and in the one God loves, Jesus Christ – Paul's words said the same thing as Abraham's story.

Jesus isn't God's contingency plan for people who can't keep promises; He's how God intended to keep both sides of the promise from the beginning. Abraham didn't know that, but he didn't need to know to take the next step in faith.

You have the whole book, from Abraham to Jesus. You can't say you don't know.

Then Jackson ended with a question I'd been asking myself since.
What's your next step?

I leaned against the wall and closed my eyes, shuffling the words on the wall in and around Abraham's story to see what they meant for me. I recalled the first page of Grandma's journal.

He said to write down what happened in the meantime, so I wouldn't forget. How could I forget seeing Jesus in a ditch? He said I'd be surprised what people forget. So, I'm writing it down.

The journal was a hopeful beginning to what would become a year of judgment and rejection. Who knows how she'd felt about it all — she wasn't one to emote on the page, and still, my mind filled in those blanks too readily. What would that year have been like for her if she hadn't written the first page?

I turned off the last light in the shop and turned the kitchen light back on. I went to the computer, closed the empty Marking Plan document, created another, and titled it, "Year One." The first three entries wrote themselves.

The first time I saw Jesus.

The first time I told someone about it.

The first time I joined a group of people talking about it.

CHAPTER 29: LU

Two weeks of easy made for a false security the day before the opening. Ted won the bet and the shop was ready at the end of two weeks. Gracie chose light-on-light for the interior with a white-gray on the walls and a natural stain on the floors. It felt sterile at first, but as the partition, shelves, and tables came in, I saw how anything darker would have made the space feel crowded. Plus, the neutral tones threaded the inventory – a crazy color palette – together.

I couldn't remember the last time something in my life had worked according to plan, but the inside of Penny Thrift was set by the time I arrived after picking up the girls from school Friday afternoon. For a moment, it was a rush of Danny and the girls running circles, Virginia shifting fabric stacks by millimeters, and Dad and Ted installing a vintage, antique brass chandelier Virginia found at an estate sale. Meanwhile Nana called out last-minute details from her notebook. Then it was over. Virginia left with Danny, and Ted left with the girls for a movie night with Gracie at their house. I drove Nana home and checked the clock when I parked the car in my parents' driveway. It was five.

Who wouldn't make pierogies at this point?

Grandma Pat made pierogies by muscle memory long before I was on the scene, and even then, I came in for the eating part. I'd worked her stand many times at the farmer's market, so I knew how to sauté them. She'd brought me in a few times for the pinching step but never for long because my pierogies always fell apart in the boiling water. But I was feeling optimistic, and by the time I got home, pierogies for everyone on opening day felt like a requirement. Like opening day wouldn't happen without them.

I set up the same three cookbooks I'd used to decipher the chicken noodle soup. The few ingredients were on-hand – potatoes, cheese, milk, butter, and salt for the filling and flour, water, oil, and salt for the dough. The recipe was less than ten steps. Make the potatoes. Mix, roll, and cut the dough. Spoon the potato in the center of the dough. Fold it. Pinch it. Boil it. Fry it in butter and onions. Eat!

Even Grandma couldn't mess with so little. Cross-referencing to compile a master recipe didn't take long. One batch made three dozen pierogies. In another burst of optimism, I multiplied the recipe times three.

I opened the large drawer that held Grandma's cache of cooking implements. To the untrained eye, it looked like a drawer of organized junk. The hand strainer she used to skim the pierogies from the top of the boiling water had sizable holes, but none so big a pierogie could fall through. The tin of the circular cutter was warped, but she corrected the imperfections to half-moons as she pinched. Why spend a dollar on a new one?

I knew all these utensils by sight, thanks to the hours I'd spent on a barstool on the other side of the buffet, talking to Grandma or doing my homework while she cooked. It was her drawer. I doubt anyone had opened it since she'd died. This thought added to the hope that a margin of her cooking mojo would transfer to me.

The first batch dashed it all. What should have been 36 finished pierogies in neat rows looked like an elementary art project, with a stockpot of mashed potatoes better suited to papier-mâché and a bowl of dough that looked like glue but without the fun smell. A smart girl would have called it quits or bought out the grocery store of frozen pierogies, but I was stupid and attempted two more batches. They turned out varying degrees of the first and were just as unusable.

I opened the cupboard to retrieve a fourth bowl, and I heard the screen door open and shut behind me. Grandma's ghost would have been helpful, but I turned around to what felt like another. It was Jackson again – not an again, like "again today" or "again this week." I saw him at church all the time, but the last time I'd seen him – really seen him – he'd stood there, and I stood here.

He held a manila envelope that he waved before placing it on the kitchen table. "Your dad asked me to drop this by."

I wouldn't have been surprised if he'd left right then, but it's not every day a person walks into a pierogie mess. I tracked his eyes as they moved from the flour in my hair and down my shirt to the floor. From there, they followed the trail to its source on the counter.

"This is quite the operation you've got going, Louisa."

I tossed him the empty bowl. He caught it and raised his eyebrows in a question. Jackson had cooked a few meals for our family last year. I didn't know if his cooking knowledge extended to pierogies, but it seemed worth a shot. He'd also manned the pierogie stand with me one Saturday last summer, so I knew he had a soft spot for them.

Those were the two official reasons for the invisible record of tonight's meeting minutes.

But the third reason was why I asked the question.

"Will you stay and help me?"

He stepped forward. "And mess with your system?"

"More like a series of misadventures. I wanted to make pierogies for Penny Thrift's re-opening tomorrow, but each bowl is worse than the last, and I can't seem to stop trying."

He glanced in the first bowl and touched the dough with his finger. "You need more flour. Flour makes things less sticky."

"So, you will help me," I said, glad my stubbornness was presenting itself in an area I found far more satisfying than making pierogies. Keeping Jackson here became top priority, and I'd play the damsel in kitchen distress card for as long as it took. He looked at his watch. I kept looking at Jackson, willing him to stay.

"How else will you prove your flour theory right?" I asked, which set his ego, at least, to work.

In 20 minutes, we had dough we could roll and cut. Worried he'd leave me to it, I brought his attention to the potatoes.

"What about these?" I asked, muscling some of the shellac onto a wooden spoon for him to see. "The texture isn't the only problem. I'm pretty sure they don't taste good."

He stuck in his finger to try, and I wrinkled my nose.

"Do you stick your finger in everything?" I asked.

"How else are you supposed to know how something tastes?"

"A spoon."

Jackson rolled his eyes but removed a spoon from the drawer. He was familiar with this kitchen. I wondered if he remembered why. I tasted potatoes from the spoon he held in front of me.

"Yup. Cement." I spit it out in the sink.

He laughed. "And you're lecturing me about tasting something with my finger. All those hours we played corn hole in your backyard when we could have been having spitting contests."

So, he did remember the hours he'd spent here. I wasn't so optimistic to think he'd accept a corn hole or spitting challenge tonight. I reached for a small container instead.

"Salt?"

"And more milk and butter."

For the next few minutes, I poured and stirred and tasted, with a clean spoon each time, until the potatoes looked and tasted like something other than building material. I added another cup of cheddar cheese to give it bite and spooned a taste for Jackson. He whistled in appreciation.

"If Grandma Pat could see you now. What do you think she'd say?"

That I should toss aside this stupid pot of potatoes and remind you of something.

"I should stay out of the kitchen," I said instead.

"Do you miss her?"

"Yes."

It came out so fast, like I'd been waiting to answer his or anyone's question about Grandma. It was a chance to talk about her. I'd been back with my family for two months, and I still felt like we were missing her. Not longing for her so much as waiting for her to come through the door. I mentally filled the void with the things I know she'd say or do, but they did little to dull her absence.

The rooms in the house felt different, too. The kitchen used to be the family stopping point because Grandma was our center, and she was always here. It was a room to watch her. It was where I would recount my day and swat away her opinions. Now, it was an extension of the hall, more a thruway from the front to the back of the house. I rarely looked at the closed door to her empty rooms.

I didn't know when Jackson had stopped cutting the dough, but he was looking at me now.

"Does re-opening Penny Thrift help or hurt?"

"Both."

"And church? I'm sure you're finding a lot about her in the history."

Grandma's diary had opened a door to a room I didn't know existed, but it was empty. My nights in the last few weeks were all about Penny Thrift, and I'd spent my days talking with people for the church project. The ones who knew Grandma always started our time with a reference to how much they admired her. Had they always felt that way? It wasn't the place to ask, but the question had created a wall all the same.

"I've found things I want to find and things I don't, Jackson."

"Do you want to talk about it?"

I shook my head as I put a tablespoonful of mashed potatoes on the first dough circle. "But I would like to know how you deal with the mess of it all."

"Can you be more specific?"

"The way church people treat other church people."

He opened his mouth to say something, hesitated, and I thought the conversation would end there. But then he stopped rolling the second batch of dough and leaned against the counter, giving me his full attention.

"I remember the mess comes from all sides, including me. My last church would say I created a lot of mess when Kate and I divorced. I did." He shrugged. "People aren't perfect."

I smacked my head in a mock epiphany.

"That's the title for the church book!"

"And how's it going?"

My face told him all he needed to know.

"You will get it done, and it will be great."

It would get done; the "great" part was debatable. Penny Thrift was the more exciting of the two projects, and I'd put my best there. For the church book, I was leaning on my high school yearbook and newspaper skills, telling myself I didn't care I was writing something I wouldn't read.

"I'm pretty sure it's going to be boring," I confessed.

"Your boring is other people's interesting."

That was sweet, and I smiled at him. He started to return it, but then his eye caught the time on the microwave behind me.

"I have to go, Louisa."

Seven on a Friday night – of course he had somewhere else to be.

"You'll be fine?" he asked, washing and drying his hands before walking to the back door. I didn't answer his question, but said something I wished I'd said a minute ago and a long time before that.

"You're doing a great job, Jackson."

He wasn't expecting the compliment, and his face showed his surprise.

"Now that I'm preaching on something less pessimistic than Ecclesiastes?"

"Those sermons changed my life."

"God's words changed your life."

"Perfect words delivered through an imperfect man and landing as God intended. Your sermons – the ones you preached here, after your church let you go, after your divorce – changed my life."

Jackson looked down, his hands in his pockets. It made for a bit of a role reversal. Usually, he brought the knowledge and I brought the critique, but I was right this time. I watched him take it in and waited for him to look back at me.

"Thank you," he said, hiding none of the emotion from his voice. Then he left.

I closed my eyes, keeping the moment close until I could no longer hear his footfalls on the deck. Whatever moment had been here – if it had existed at all – was gone, leaving me with dozens of pierogies in various stages of undress. My new plan was to throw them all away.

"Need some help, kiddo?"

I jumped at Dad's voice from the other side of the kitchen. He looked from me to the mess to the envelope Jackson had put on the table. I wondered how long he'd been standing there.

"I didn't mean to interrupt, but I knew Jackson was coming by and ..."

"How much did you hear?"

He crossed the kitchen.

"Enough to be proud of you."

Dad didn't say anything else or ask questions, but he hugged me. Then he offered again to help me.

We settled into an efficient rhythm and made our way through filling and pinching a batch before Mom entered the way Jackson left – through the back-screen door, but with a bag.

"What's that?" I asked her.

"Dinner. I'll get it started and help you finish while it cooks."

Mom joined us for the final stage – managing the pierogies in and out of the boiling water so they'd be ready to sauté tomorrow. Out of nowhere, she started laughing and turned to Dad.

"Remember when I tried to get to know your mom by making pierogies with her?"

He laughed, too. "You definitely got to know her."

I knew the story of how my parents met – Dad worked at the summer resort where Mom's family had a lake house. I didn't know much of what happened after, but of course Mom, like any other girl, would have wanted to impress her boyfriend's mom.

"Why did you choose the cooking route?" I asked. It's not like Nana Bea would have raised her to work in the kitchen. They hired people for that sort of thing.

"Because it was all the woman did, other than sew. I couldn't fake even stitches, so helping her with pierogies seemed like my best option."

Dad started laughing all over again. "She bossed you from start to finish."

"And ended by saying I'd never be able to cook for her son – in other words, 'I should probably leave now.'"

"That sounds pretty harsh, even for Grandma," I said.

"She grew into a manageable feisty. When I met her, she was mostly insulting. What she was like before that, I don't want to think about.

"Well, I think you won in the end. You got Dad."

"Yes, but Grandma Pat was right. I couldn't cook. Then she moved in and took care of it for me."

"Did you mind her taking over your kitchen?"

"No."

Mom took a minute and looked around. I wondered if she saw what I saw and felt what I felt in here.

"But I guess I never really thought about it as mine."

CHAPTER 30: JACKSON

I was 15 minutes late to Rebecca's house for dinner, a detail she wouldn't normally notice, except she was hosting friends. I parked behind their car and did my best to put the last hour out of my mind as I walked to the front door.

Rebecca smiled when she saw me. "A flour traffic jam, Jackson?"

I looked down. It was not a good time to be wearing a dark blue shirt. I kissed Rebecca's cheek before turning to introduce myself to her friends, David and Susan. Rebecca had grown up with them and was the maid of honor in their wedding.

"It was worth the wait, so long as you brought whatever made the mess," Susan said as I shook her hand.

"Jackson's a great cook." Rebecca led us to her kitchen table, which was ready to go, down to the lit candlesticks. "What were you making?"

"Pierogies." I had a question at the ready to move us along, but David beat me to it.

"What are those?"

I coughed. "It's a Polish thing – dough wrapped around mashed potatoes or another type of filling."

"Is it a family recipe?"

His friendliness felt like I was being cornered. "Not mine. I was helping a friend make a bunch for a store re-opening tomorrow. When did you two get in today?"

Their answer moved us to another topic, but a sentence too late, Rebecca's eyes told me. The rest of dinner was friendly enough, though it felt like a countdown to me, and my suspicion was confirmed as soon as Rebecca said goodbye to her friends. She closed the door and turned on me.

"You came late to dinner at my place, a dinner I've been cooking since I left work, because you were helping her?"

"I didn't know you wanted help."

"That's not the point."

I stepped toward her and put my hands on her shoulders. Rebecca shrugged them off. I tried again, holding her steady this time.

"Is the point that I was late or that I was with Louisa?'

"Both and in the opposite order – that being with her made you late to me."

"That's me not looking at the clock, Rebecca."

She met my gaze. "Is it, Jackson?"

"Louisa asked me to help."

Rebecca stepped around me and called over her shoulder as she headed to the kitchen. "I bet she did."

I closed my eyes to the sound of Rebecca slamming plates in the dishwasher. I could go in there. I could offer to help, but I might get a plate to the head. I sat on the couch, waiting it out.

Five minutes stretched to thirty, and felt like forever until she left the kitchen. She came no farther than the entry to her living room.

"Do you want to be with me, Jackson?"

I nodded. She looked down.

"And if I told you I can't handle you hanging out with her? What would you say then?"

"This is the second time since she came back. The first I told you about – for us to settle everything from before. Tonight was a coincidence."

I crossed the room, not sure if she'd respond by backing away, but she leaned against the wall and looked at me.

"You didn't answer my question, Jackson."

"Is that what you want – that if I find myself in the same place as Louisa, I leave as quickly as possible?"

She spread her hands. "No, it's not what I want. I want to be stronger than that. But it might be what I need. I'm going to think about it."

I nodded. "And if you don't want to go to the opening of her shop tomorrow, it's okay. We can stay away."

"And miss your pierogies?"

I leaned toward her, and she didn't move away. I put my hands on her waist. She put her hands on my shoulders, and I kissed her. I meant it. I was also relieved she hadn't given me an ultimatum.

139

CHAPTER 31: LU

It's amazing how what takes weeks to plan takes a few hours to run its course.

Opening Day ran like Wedding Fest, but this time we wouldn't pack it up and congratulate ourselves on a successful one-and-done. This time, I wouldn't return on Monday to a boss who would tell me I was out of a job.

Because I was the boss and Penny Thrift wouldn't be open on Mondays at all. Given each stakeholder's day jobs, we'd decided on a Wednesday – Saturday operation.

Opening Day hinted at how it could build over time. First, Virginia needed to raise her prices or sew faster because she sold out her fashion and home lines halfway through the afternoon. I wished the quilts were as popular, but maybe that was because choosing fabrics and quilt designs took longer than people felt like they had at the event. There was a lot going on – a lot of bodies, a lot of noise, and a lot of activity. Many of the vendors let the customers participate in building what they bought, like Emily's flower bar. These were more popular than the booths with static buys and reinforced the draw of interactive workshops.

Products made well, with purpose and artistry, inspired people to either buy or create. I was excited to see how Penny Thrift would fill both sides of this line. But this was all brainstorming for next week. On Opening Day, I fed off the energy.

I'd started the day nervous, having no job other than to "circulate," according to my family. I'd envisioned this as an awkward game of social pinball where I'd greet people, ask if they needed anything, and make noxious small talk.

But Penny Thrift wasn't normal retail, and I wasn't an anonymous worker. I was Pat Sokolowski's granddaughter and within the first five minutes of opening, a long-time customer found me and told me a story of how Grandma helped her choose the fabrics for her first quilt. Another woman followed, and by the time the fourth woman found me, I'd stolen Nana's notebook and pen so I could write their stories down. Each was a facet. Whether Penny Thrift would go on to succeed felt beside the point compared to what Grandma had already done. The more stories I heard, the more I saw how today was as much a celebration of a life's work as a beginning.

Nana's silver pen was beautiful, smooth, and heavy. After a couple hours of writing, my hand was shaking. Also, I'd forgotten to eat lunch again and remembering made the rest of me feel a little shaky. I needed food, and I needed quiet. I was on the front lawn and took the longer, quieter way around the side of the house to get to the back door.

I peeked into the detached garage as I went. When Ted finished the interior renovation with a week to spare, Gracie had assigned him to a brainchild of her own. I hadn't thought about it, but of course she would. People coming would have kids and wouldn't it be great if the kids had a space where they'd be allowed to touch something? She asked Ted to clear out the detached garage, and her girls made signs, posted along the driveway for "Kids' Creator Market, This Way." The inside was tables lined with the old fabric I wanted gone and Virginia wanted for "something." I didn't stop as I passed the garage, but I could see the kids were doing something, a lot of things. The garage was full of scrapped masterpieces and kids, including my nieces, having fun with Gracie sitting in the middle of it all.

The kitchen was empty, and most people made their cupcake run a long time ago. There were a few left and many, many ugly pierogies. More for me, and I topped them with a heaping spoon of sour cream.

I sat in the strange avocado green chair/stepstool that had always occupied the corner of Penny Thrift's kitchen between the fridge and the wall. No one would look for me here. I turned every sense but taste down as I alternated bites of savory and sweet. The crowd on the other side of the wall became a hum, and I felt my body slow down. I closed my eyes – maybe not the smartest move because at one point, I dolloped buttercream frosting instead of sour cream on my pierogie.

The food was gone before I was ready to reenter the fray, and I sat a bit longer with the notebook open, skimming the stories and prepping myself to discover more. One came unbidden.

"They look cute together," a woman said from across the kitchen. She stood with another woman in the entryway between the kitchen and the shop, their backs to me. I couldn't tell who "they" were from my vantage point.

She could be talking about anyone, I told myself, it didn't have to be …

"Rebecca is a great fit for him. I bet they'll be engaged before the summer is out."

I closed my eyes to drive out the words, but the image of Jackson and Rebecca when they first arrived replaced them. They did look cute. I'd smiled at them from across the lawn. I saw his hand holding hers, and then I looked away. Today was for satisfaction, not wanting more.

I shouldn't have to hear these words. And there were more.

"She'll make a great pastor's wife."

Everything slowed down after that. The women moved from the doorway, but their words stayed. I slowly stood up, not wanting to go in the middle of the room where the words lingered and definitely not wanting to go into the shop where the cute couple was. I thought about the garage and Gracie, but what if Rebecca made her way there? Then I'd be stuck watching her be awesome with kids. I saw two cupcakes left on the counter. What if those were the ones Jackson and Rebecca were about to come into the kitchen and eat? Then I'd be stuck watching two cute people eat cupcakes.

I crossed the kitchen, popped one in my mouth and was peeling the paper off the second when Virginia entered.

"Oh, good. I'm glad you're getting something to eat. After you're done, can you help me bring something up from the basement?"

I said I was happy to, except I wasn't. It didn't help that I berated myself for it. Unhappiness and anger are a bad mix, and they created a fog between me and everyone I spoke with the rest of the afternoon. I doubt anyone noticed, but I was glad when the last guest left, and another round of work took over. I didn't have another fake smile in me.

At this point it was my family, Roddy, and me. The tasks were many and distinct. Break down tables and haul them to the truck. Pick up trash. Close the garage door. Sweep the shop floor. Dad ordered pizza from Creek's, which everyone appreciated, but me. My three cupcakes had reformed in the pit of my stomach. Also, it reminded me of breaking down Fest last year. We'd had Creek's then, too, but Jackson was there. The memory felt mean. I felt mean, which kicked off more ruminating.

My family left, and I was about to follow, but I remembered Nana's notebook in the basement. If I was going to spend tonight alone in my room, I wanted these stories to keep me company. Maybe they could drive out the one I kept spinning in my mind.

I opened the door to the stairs and heard the end of the second conversation not meant for me today. I'd thought I was alone, but Roddy and Virginia were down there. I didn't catch what he'd said, but from her response, I could guess.

"I'm not interested in dinner or anything else, Roddy."

She looked up and saw me, but she wasn't finished. She looked Roddy straight in the eyes and kept her words simple, so there would be no misunderstanding.

"Seeing you reminds me of how I used to be, and I'm not that person anymore. I wish you would stop coming around."

She climbed the stairs and didn't look at me as she left. I sunk to the top step, burying my face in my hands. What a day. I looked back up, and Roddy stood in the same place.

He looked at me. I don't know if he'd registered my presence until then, and he walked up the stairs, stopping once his eyes were level with mine. His face didn't reveal anything. When he spoke, his tone was light.

"Do you want to get out of here?

CHAPTER 32: LU

A bar with drinks for him and food for me was how Roddy pitched it. The place was on the same street as the new coffee shop in the depot and carried that vibe of something new made from something old – in this case, a converted gas station. It was a beautiful night, and the garage doors were up to bring the outside in. The food was good. My party dress fit the scene, and the hum of others' conversations filled the space, exempting Roddy and me from adding to it.

I ate. He drank, and I counted, unconsciously at first. By the time I finished my pasta, he'd downed four.

I put my fork and knife on the plate and pushed it a few inches in front of me. By the time I put my hands on my lap I had his attention. I smiled.

"Let me get the check as a thank you for helping to make today happen."

Roddy shook his head. "I'll take care of it."

I exhaled, mentally circling how the next half hour could go. Ten minutes to get the check and pay, another couple minutes to walk through the restaurant to the car, and ten minutes for Roddy to drive me across town to Penny Thrift to get my car. Going home an hour ago seemed like a loser option. Now, I wanted to be home by nine.

I went to the restroom and returned to the table. Roddy wasn't there. The crowd around the bar was two circles deep, and when I found him, he was sitting next to a woman I didn't know. She looked at me like I was a problem, but the real problem was the next drink in Roddy's hand.

"Did you get the check?"

He shook his head.

"I'd like to go home now," I said.

"Because you have someone waiting for you there?"

The woman next to Roddy smirked. I put my hand on his arm.

"I'm going to give you the benefit of the doubt …"

"I wouldn't," he said, cutting me off.

His glass was half full, but he tossed it back in one swallow and waived to the bartender for another. I shook my head at the bartender, stopping him before he turned. Roddy's look to me was cold. He took his keys out of his pocket and handed them to me.

"You can take yourself home, Lu."

"I can't drive stick shift."

"I guess you'll have to figure something else out."

He signaled to the bartender again and turned back to the woman. I pocketed the keys and stepped back from the bar to think about my options, but they all involved me leaving and Roddy staying, unless I called Ted or Jackson to haul Roddy out of here. I didn't want to call Ted; he'd just started to open his mind about Roddy. Seeing him like this would undo a month's work. And Jackson? I didn't want to call Jackson.

I took to the periphery at a lone stool where the end of the bar met the patio. I could track Roddy from here, and there were enough people in between us that he wouldn't know. I'd seen plenty of drunks in my law firm party days with John. It went one of two ways. I was hoping Roddy was the type to go quiet.

I reached into my purse for a book and my hand found the one from the bookstore – *Gently Flows Her Heart*. I looked at the woman on the cover. She was blonde and wore her hair in a bun. I pulled mine into a similar, messier version with a tie from my purse and settled in to read what she had to say.

I made it five chapters before Roddy got into it with another man from the bar. By the time I texted Jackson to get us and made my way back to Roddy, both men were standing, and the woman Roddy had been sitting next to was behind the other man.

I stepped in between both with Roddy behind me and this man's chest at my line of sight. I looked up and smelled stale breath before seeing the eyes of a man about to lose it.

"He's with me," I said with enough of a tone of apology to move us along. The man opened his mouth to argue, but I was faster. "And we're leaving."

I didn't have to ask for the check this time; the bartender was ready. I handed him my credit card and clamped my hands to Roddy's arms to move him as far away from the angry man as possible. There was an empty table for two next to the hostess stand. I maneuvered Roddy into one seat and took the other. If anything had registered from the almost fight, Roddy's expression didn't show it. He smiled.

"I thought you left. Have you been having a good time?"

"If you call reading at the other end of the bar while keeping an eye on you and stopping a fight a good time, sure."

The smile left his face. "I had it under control. I can take care of myself."

"Not when you're drunk."

"I'm not drunk."

"So … what? Five drinks an hour is a normal day for you?"

He patted his pockets.

"I have your keys, Roddy."

He reached out his hand, and I shook my head.

"Give me the keys. It's time to go," he said.

"As your friend …"

"Like hell you are. You have a stick up your ass, you know that?"

He leaned, his face a few inches from mine, and I shouted right back.

"Because I don't want to be here? I asked you to take me home over an hour ago, but you decided to get another drink and hit on someone else's girl. I'm not sure what's triggered you tonight, maybe it's what Virginia said, but I don't deserve to be on the other end of it."

Roddy slammed his hand on the table before grabbing my wrist — strong, but not meant to hurt. He looked into my eyes, in a way that made me wonder if he'd realized who he was talking to until this moment.

"This is my life, Lu."

He started to stand, but he didn't have the capacity. He fell back in his chair and rubbed his hand across his face, closing his eyes. Then he folded his arms on the table and put his head down.

I was angry, but I saw him. Maybe for the first time, I really saw him – not as Jackson's friend, not as a person I thought was my friend, and not as the man who answered every question I'd asked him over the last two months.

He needed a glass of water. I mouthed my request to the nearest server, sat back and waited for Jackson.

CHAPTER 33: JACKSON

Her text was simple. Roddy's drunk. I need you to come get him.

Roddy and I had spent more time together in the last few weeks than we had in years, and I'd been seeing some changes, especially in how he was helping Louisa get the store running. But I knew Roddy, and I had to battle my instincts on the drive.

She was sitting next to him at a small table when I got there.

"Are you okay?" I asked, searching her face for any signs that might say otherwise.

"I'm fine."

She stood, and I leaned down to get Roddy, who was slumped over the table. It took him a few seconds to come to and then a few more to realize what was happening. His eyes went from me to Louisa.

"Well aren't you two a pair." He said it slow and sarcastic.

"Knock it off. You should be thanking her."

"For what? I've gotten myself this far without her help."

There's no arguing with a drunk person, and it was hard enough to prop up someone who didn't think he needed it. Somehow, I got him through the front door and into my car, with Roddy muttering the whole way.

I shut the door and turned to Louisa. "Did he say something about a fight?"

She shrugged. "More like an almost fight."

I opened the passenger door for her, but she shook her head.

"I thought it'd be best if you took him straight home. My dad is coming to get me."

I closed the door and walked to the driver's side. She leaned against the roof of the car.

"You know Roddy better than I do, and I'm not saying I know what he needs right now, but …"

She shook her head, her eyes looking past me into whatever had happened here. She focused them again on me after a few seconds.

"I'm angry with him. He earned it, but I think what he needs is compassion. Think about it."

I did on the drive back to his place, about a half hour out of town. We didn't say anything to each other, and as soon as we stopped, Roddy left the car and walked into the house. Tonight probably wasn't the time the deal with this, but I got out anyway and walked toward the garage.

The first time I'd slept over at Roddy's when we were kids, I'd been nervous. His parents lived in the only gated community in town. Seeing my dad, the best man I knew, have to speak to a guard before we could gain access to the road leading to my friend's house didn't help. I was convinced my good behavior wouldn't be good enough.

Their family of three greeted us at the door. You could fit my parents' house in their entryway, but Roddy's dad dominated the setting. He filled every room he took us to on the house tour – a requirement of my dad's before he'd drop me off anywhere – but I think Roddy's dad would have done it anyway. He liked to impress. He was impressive, the house was impressive, and at dinner, he did his best to show me his son was impressive. A 10-year-old boy doesn't care how much his friend knows, but Roddy's dad grilled him when he wasn't relaying to me what Roddy had done on the football and baseball fields. The play-by-play didn't bother me; the thought I'd be recruited for a scrimmage in the backyard after dinner did. Thankfully, Roddy's parents had somewhere to be, and his grandma came to watch us. It was a normal sleepover after that, but in a basement with a crazy amount of toys.

Roddy's dad filled the house the next time I slept over, but in a different way. Only Roddy came to greet us, and he came straight to the car. He was smooth, even back then, and it wasn't until my dad pulled out of the drive and we got to the front door I realized his conversation with my dad – asking about his day, telling him about our plan for the night – was a cover. He smiled and waved to my dad from the front door, and as soon as he was out of sight, he turned to me.

"We need to go in through the kitchen door, Jack. My dad is asleep, and I don't want to wake him. I already took some food down to the basement, and we'll stay down there all night. Okay?"

Sure. I wanted to play with the most extensive micro-machine play set I'd ever seen outside of a toy store. And maybe Roddy's dad was asleep when we got there, but for the rest of the night he was in and out. When he was in, he was loud. A couple times he shouted for Roddy, who'd freeze, as if his Dad could see him through the floor. He'd wait, and I wondered for what, but then I'd hear his mom's voice – softer, insistent, which redirected the shouting to her.

The pattern repeated through the night, and I'd never been so excited for the early sleepover pick-up before church. I told my dad about it as soon as I got in the car because he would know what to do. Dad didn't let problems simmer. He went to Roddy's house that afternoon. I knew my Dad well enough to know how the conversation went. He'd be polite. He'd relay the facts of what I'd said, but without judgment or emotion. He would ask Roddy's dad if he had anything to add. He would ask for assurances, but he wouldn't accept excuses. Then he would make a decision best suited for everyone involved.

Of course, all Dad told me was the decision part. There would be no more sleepovers at Roddy's. I was allowed to play there after school until his dad came home from work, but Roddy and I hung out at my house after that.

There were two sides to Roddy – one who played by the rules to excellence when it served him and one who broke them every time they didn't. The second side coped with the pressure of the first, and as we grew up, it'd gone from adventurous to reckless to wrong.

I walked in through the door from the garage, which opened into a hallway with a laundry room and bathroom on either side. From here everything opened into a giant room with the kitchen, living area, and dining room squared around a freestanding stone fireplace rising to the highest point in the cathedral ceiling.

The house was quiet and the space was full. So many empty bottles – on the tables and scattered around the floor, not to mention plates of half-finished food and trash everywhere but the empty trashcan in the kitchen.

I'd been in this place once. He'd built it right before I moved back, and he was proud to show me around. I was proud of him, too. He'd overcome his father's business failures. He'd earned this house, but I remember thinking it was a lot of house for one person. It felt lonely then. It felt desolate now.

I started cleaning up, making that my plan for the night, but Roddy emerged from his room a couple hours later. He'd showered and looked impossibly awake, whereas I had no idea how I was going to preach later this morning.

Roddy came over, and we hauled the trash to the garage. He closed the lid and followed me to my car.

"Say it," he said as I opened my door.

"No."

"Are you trying to make me feel worse?"

"I'm taking a page from your playbook this time, from when you helped me move after Kate left. Also, I think this is what Louisa was prompting me to do before she went home."

He nodded, looking at the ground before looking at me. "She's special. I'm not sure what I was trying to prove last night, and I didn't mean for it to involve her, but then it did and …

"Listen to yourself. You're not taking responsibility for the position you put her in. Last night was a small part of what's going on with you, Roddy, and you know it."

He'd never talked about what went on in his home growing up; he only referenced it. Until now, I'd respected the boundary, but I didn't want him to start re-filling the space I'd just cleared with more bottles.

"You don't have to be your dad," I said. I'd thought this so many times. It felt good to say it. I wanted him to hear it.

"Easy for you to say, Jack, when you have a dad like yours."

"My dad is a good man, but growing up as a pastor's kid has its own pressures. There were a lot of eyes on me all the time. There still are."

"I didn't know."

"Because you didn't ask." I took a breath and put my hand on his shoulder. "But I never asked you, either. I'm sorry."

He responded with a hand to my shoulder, giving me the most apologetic look I'd ever seen from him.

"I'm sorry. My father's drinking ruined our family. I don't live with anyone, and I've kept my drinking here since I built this place.

That was how I broke the cycle in my own weird way, but then tonight happened. I see now I'm not the only one affected. I'd like to say this won't happen again – with her or me or any of it."

I opened my car door, then looked back at Roddy's house. He'd done this alone, and he lived here alone. Grace was a word he would have learned in parochial school, but there was nothing from his past to show him what it meant.

"If you're serious about changing, starting with the drinking, you're going to need help."

"You will help me?"

"You're going to need more than my help."

"But you would help me?"

I stepped forward again, this time to hug him.

"I will."

CHAPTER 34: LU

I stayed in bed until I heard my parents leave for church on Sunday. I went downstairs, made coffee, drank it, and fell back asleep. When I came downstairs later that afternoon, Mom told me Nana had called, asking about her notebook. There was no rush, but I took it to her anyway.

It seemed like I drove Nana to something or other a few times a week, but she was usually waiting for me when I got to her house. I hadn't been inside since I took her to Penny Thrift the first time. The dresser was still in the middle of the foyer. I remembered my initial barter – a store for a turquoise dresser. I could still use the dresser. Earlier this week, I'd duct taped my top drawer to keep it from bottoming out.

I ran my hand along the surface. Grandma Pat had sanded it smooth before she painted. I pulled out the top drawer, surprised at the weight. I didn't know much about wood other than good wood was heavy and cheap wood was light. You stained the good and painted the cheap, my dad had told me. This dresser was paint on heavy.

The drawers were empty, and I was pushing in the last one when Nana came in. I handed her the notebook and watched her skim some of the stories. She closed it after a few minutes and looked at me.

"I am proud of you, Lu."

Grandma Pat would have been proud, and she would have told me a dozen things I should have done differently. Her good opinions paired with her critiques, and she'd poured out both all the time.

Nana portioned her compliments. If there was a way to close out yesterday for me, this was it.

"Thank you, Nana."

"Did you have a good time?"

"I am proud of what we did, but there were other things that happened I wish hadn't."

I took a breath, wiping my palms along my thighs. Nana sat next to me.

"I overheard people talking about Rebecca and Jackson – what a cute couple they make. It's true."

I looked at her for confirmation, but she didn't move.

"She won't mess up with him like I did."

"It's not just a mess, and it's not just your mess."

"That doesn't change that she's with Jackson, and I am not."

"No."

"Did you know about Grandma?"

If I didn't ask now, I wouldn't. Nana seemed confused at first by the topic change, but something in her eyes looked too wary for her not to know what I was asking about. She worded her question carefully.

"What about Pat?"

"I found an old journal of hers in the basement of Penny Thrift. It covers her first year after Jesus and the ditch. The way she would talk about it to me was as if her switch into a different life was instantaneous."

"And what does the journal say?"

"That people in the church were stuck on who she'd been. They talked and threw up some stops. She wasn't wanted."

"This surprises you?"

"The hypocrisy in general? No. That's just people. But it upsets me, and it doesn't sync with what I know. Her funeral was packed. I spent most of yesterday recording the stories people shared about how wonderful she was. Dad said people were honored she left them her old stuff after she died. The dresser she left you is still standing in the middle of your foyer.

"I know it's from a long time ago, and maybe everyone changed, but it's disappointing, and it doesn't help with this fear I have that church people are a shade different from everyone else. How can you change if people only remember who you were? Why would you talk about it? Who would believe it?"

"It's not a maybe, Lu," Nana said.

"What?"

"You said, 'maybe everyone changed.' It's not a maybe. People did change. Pat changed."

She stood up and walked to the middle of the room, stopping at the dresser.

"You asked about my first impressions of your grandma, and our first meeting went like I told you. We didn't run in the same circles, and I didn't want us to run in the same circles. I knew who she was. It's a small town. People talk and stories get around. Your mom was set on marrying your father, and I couldn't change that, so I settled on throwing the biggest wedding I could.

"Of course, Pat would have none of it. The country club wasn't her style. She'd also never read the rulebook concerning mothers-of-the-groom. She kept coming around, refusing to remain uninvolved and fighting every choice. She insisted on footing half the bill, which just wasn't done."

"What did you do?"

She raised an eyebrow. "I showed her a portion of the receipts, of course. I kept the secret until the morning of the wedding, when it was apparent her 'half' accounted for a fraction of what was there.

"Pat didn't say anything, and the wedding and the reception went off perfectly. Your mom and dad left, and the guests trickled away. Your grandfather left to pull around the car, and all I had to do was say goodbye to Pat. I hoped I wouldn't have to see her again until Thanksgiving.

"That's when she told me I'd made a fool of her. I denied it. She said I was in denial. I denied that, too."

Nana saw my smile and returned it.

"It is humorous, looking back. Then she saw your grandfather drive up. Pat said, 'You know he messes around, right? Not with many, just with the one woman, and I know her.'"

I wasn't expecting that, and I put my hand to my chest, channeling my energy from breathing to rewinding through what I knew about my family. I was little when Grandfather died. The memories were kind, but typical of a granddaughter. He was the man who would sneak me ice cream cones when Nana laid down for her afternoon nap.

No, if there was anything to clue into right now, it was Nana's narration. I looked at her, standing with perfect posture next to a turquoise dresser and speaking with the even tone she used for everything. I suspected what she was telling me now she'd composed a long time ago but never shared.

Nana took a breath and continued. "I reacted like you'd expect. I was raised in a world where we don't talk about such things, at least not to the people who are affected by them. It's poor form, and maybe even worse than the cheating itself."

"So, you didn't respond?"

"I said goodbye."

"What about to Grandfather?"

"No."

"But ..."

"No, Lu."

She held up her hand, her tone firm from a decision she'd made – maybe on the ride home with him that night. "It wasn't something I wanted to verify, and if I had, it wouldn't have changed anything, including how I felt. I loved your grandfather. And then he up and died, without warning and without time to clear out his dresser."

She opened the top drawer and followed the wood grain with her finger.

"This was his dresser. I went in to his room the afternoon he died to find clothes to lay him out in for the funeral. Sitting there, right on top of the undershirts in the top drawer was a picture of him and her. I knew it by how he was smiling at her, and in such a way ..."

Her thoughts took over her words, and she shifted her eyes from the drawer. She didn't need the picture in front of her to see it.

"I sat on the edge of his bed and looked at the picture for the rest of the day. The phone rang and people knocked at the door, but I kept looking at the picture. Pat was the first one to find me. We'd kept it polite in the years since the wedding, but we barely talked. She sat next to me on the bed like we were friends, and I handed her the picture and asked for the woman's name.

Nana gave a short a laugh. "She wouldn't tell me. Maybe it was the first time she'd ever withheld information. I could have pushed for it, but I'm glad I didn't. I wouldn't want to know now. I told her I didn't want the dresser in my house. She told me she'd take care of it. Then she packed a bag for me and took me to your house, and you know the rest. I lived there until she died last year."

Nana reached into the drawer, removing a small sheet of paper taped to the inside of the top.

"In all my weekly visits back here to collect my clothes, I never opened the door to your grandfather's room again. I didn't know she'd kept and repainted the dresser until your father brought it over after she died. Inside was this."

She brought it over, and I saw one verse – Isaiah 43:19 – written in grandma's chicken scratch:

See, I am doing a new thing! Now it springs up; do you not perceive it? I am making a way in the wilderness and streams in the wasteland.

I turned the paper around in my hands, reading the verse from all angles. Nana sat next to me.

"It's her strange sense of humor and a touch dramatic, to be sure, but what she did with this dresser and how she left it to me was who she was. We rarely agreed on anything, your grandma and me, but we were on the same side from that afternoon. Pat was the best woman I knew, but she wasn't perfect – not before Jesus and the ditch and not after. She needed to learn to stop speaking every thought that came into her head, and if she was going to say the hard things, she needed to learn tact. I like to think I helped her with that.

"She helped me, too. You probably don't remember, but right after I moved in, I only left the house to come here or go to church, but your family's church instead of the one your grandfather and I were married in. I couldn't stand the thought that people there may have known and talked, but never to me. Pat put up with my seclusion for a year before she started responding to invitations on my behalf. She went to all of them with me, so that made it okay."

Nana stopped, and I waited for the next chapter. I looked from the paper, to the dresser, and back to her. After a minute when she didn't say anything more, I realized she was done. The woman needed to work on her endings.

"So, all of this is to say …"

"It doesn't all say one thing, Lu. It says many things, and you take from it what you will as you will, like I do. You can't change the past. You can't stop people from talking. The best you can do is live your life."

That was a better ending. I handed her the verse and watched her fold it according to the seams. Then, I just watched her. Nana always changed her clothes after church, but someone who didn't know better would think she hadn't gotten around to it because her dressed-down was flats with a skirt and sweater set. This had always made her a touch too fancy for our house. On the outside, she fit better in this foyer, but I wondered whether she'd outgrown it, too.

She stood up, ready to be done with this conversation. I was ready for another nap.

"You don't have to stay here, you know," I said as we walked to the door.

"I've been thinking about that, but it's going to take some time to figure out. I've never chosen a place by myself before." She opened the door. "And it's okay if it takes you time to figure out your next step. How long has it been since I moved into your place and back here? Sixteen years?"

"This is no longer helpful, Nana."

"Well when you make a decision, I have a dresser waiting for you."

I smiled, thankful she'd made one for me.

CHAPTER 35: LU

I didn't take a nap but went straight into Grandma's rooms when I got home. They were empty, as I'd often pictured, but the feelings I'd associated with these pictures didn't come. It felt good to open the door from the kitchen, and I kept going, opening the French doors that led from the sitting room to the deck and the two windows that looked to the backyard from the bedroom.

The suite was less square footage than my attic bedroom, but it suited me, and I already had a piece of furniture to go in here. When I saw Dad cross through the kitchen, I called to him and asked if he could haul the dresser back from Nana's in his truck sometime this week. He walked over, the smile big on his face as he looked at me sitting cross-legged in the middle of the floor. He nodded but didn't say a word.

Mom was quieter about it. In the absence of prepping a store for opening, I remembered that Sundays at home were for meandering. It was interesting to spy her patterns – working a bit in the mulch beds around the deck to reading on the deck, then getting a glass of water before heading back to the mulch beds, but turning before she got to the deck stairs to go somewhere else in the house. I sneaked looks at all her pivots, and at one point, caught her doing the same with me, though I hadn't moved from my seat on the sitting room floor. An hour later, she came to the door.

"Is that Penny Thrift work or church work?" she asked in reference to the notebook on my lap and the other papers I'd laid in a semi-circle around me.

"Church work."

"The celebration is a few weeks away, right? Are you almost finished?"

"Yes and no. I could send what I have to the printer tomorrow, but it's not good."

"How do you know the changes you're working on are any better?" It was more of a curious question than a critical one.

I shrugged. "I'm less bored by it."

"And you're working on it in here because ..."

"Because I'm thinking about moving into Grandma's rooms."

I paused, realizing my assumption once I said it. She and Dad had hosted me longer than their fair share. I wouldn't blame them if they wanted their 28-year-old daughter out and the house to themselves.

I looked from the revised outline for the church book to Mom, wondering if she knew why Nana moved in all of those years ago. Probably, but I doubted she would have heard about it from Nana first. Mom never mentioned it to me; it wasn't my place to bring it up now. Instead, I asked the question that was starting to make me nervous.

"Would you be okay with me living with you for a while longer, Mom?"

She nodded and turned. Then she surprised me by turning back.

"I've been so anxious you'd leave town again. I don't think I've seen how much you're trying to settle in this time." She smiled. "Your father wants you here. I want you here. It feels more like home when you're here."

I hadn't been so caught by work since the article I wrote for *NYNY*. Opening a store was a different sort of work – an unknown gamble with a steep learning curve. There'd been no rest for my mind in the last few weeks because every day carried doubt, sometimes fear. I was glad the opening went well, but was still astonished it had. I wouldn't know how to tell someone else to do it; I didn't know if I would have been able to repeat it.

Writing was a different kind of hard, but one that returned my energy as I expended it. I'd been writing for a long time, and it was nice to be back in a place where I didn't have to first text Roddy, look at Virginia's drawings, refer to Grandma's records, or wait for Ted to do his part. I knew what to do with a blank sheet of paper. I knew a good story begins with discovery, and in looking over my notes, I saw I'd gone wrong from the start with this project. I'd worked without expectation. I'd observed without seeing. I had mundane answers because I'd asked mundane questions. Nothing interesting comes from a writer uninterested in her work.

The last 24 hours reminded me there's a lot more going on, especially with the people who seem "normal." They have stories, and for the people I'd met over the last few weeks, church was part of their stories. But how and why and for what? A woman has reasons for why she chooses to go to church on a Sunday morning, and I smiled, remembering mine from last summer – a mix of Jackson, cake, and a conversation that opened me up when I thought I had closed down.

There's a why behind the first time a woman carries a sermon with her long past a Sunday morning.

What makes her come back?

What compels her to stay?

I should have asked these questions. I wrote better ones now.

My parents offered to take me out for a celebratory dinner of Penny Thrift's opening, but I took a rain check to make a plan for how I'd revise this book and get it to the printer in time for the church anniversary in a few weeks. When I heard a knock on the front door, I was surprised to see an hour had passed since my parents left. The doorbell and another knock followed. I left my new rooms for the first time that afternoon, the short walk through the kitchen and hallway working out the kinks from sitting too long.

I opened the door to Roddy. I closed the door behind me and leaned against it, looking at him. Last night seemed far away. I'd chosen not to think about it, and I wasn't ready to deal with him.

"What are you doing here?"

"I'm here to teach you how to drive stick shift."

"Is this supposed to be some sort of apology?"

"No." He stepped closer and took off his sunglasses. "I'm sorry, Lu. I should have taken you home when you asked. Much as I would like to say I would never have let anything happen, we both know I wasn't capable of keeping that promise last night."

I nodded. It was a good start.

"I also said some things to you. I don't remember what they were, but I know they were mean."

I opened my mouth to cut Roddy off, not wanting to rehash any of it, but he held up his hand.

"Let me say this – that was my anger for me and my world. It looks nothing like yours, and what I said has nothing to do with you. My father is a drunk. He has pushed me hard my whole life. My mom relies on me like a woman should rely on her husband, not her son. Everything I do, which I realize might look impressive, is to spite them."

He took a breath. "How am I doing so far?"

I folded my arms across my chest. "Keep going."

"Helping you these last couple months is the first time I've helped someone other than myself in a long time. It also made me think I could be different, but Virginia saw through me last night. That's not an excuse, but it explains the trigger. As you can see, it doesn't take much.

"I don't know if I can change. I don't know if when I wake up tomorrow I will want to, but ..."

At this point, he looked down and then looked back at me, like a confession was coming.

"I've moved in with Jackson."

"Never a dull moment with you." I laughed in disbelief. There was so much to unpack with this new information, but I started with the math. "I've never been to your place, but I'm sure it's massive. I bet you could fit his rental into your living room."

"Which is what I told him."

"And?"

"The pastor is unmoved. He's out right now, and he gave me two options: stay at his place or come apologize to you. I'm doing one better." He dangled the keys in front of me again. "I think it's time you learned how to drive stick, on the off-chance you find yourself across from an asshole who refuses to take you home."

It was too many emotions for one day, but I rolled with the one I felt now – ready for a break from all the thinking. I took the keys and walked to the car.

"It's like an early birthday present," I said.

"And when is that?"

"This Saturday. What if I scratch your car?"

"You won't scratch my car."

"But if I do?" I persisted, opening the driver's side door and looking at him over the hood.

I stalled before we got out of the driveway. I think it caused him physical pain, but he didn't say anything. I patted his hand and smiled.

"Don't you worry, Roddy. If anything happens, I'll loan you my Civic."

CHAPTER 36: LU

29.

My new age flashed in my mind as clearly as the red numbers on my alarm clock. I'd turned it off last night in honor of the occasion, so why was I waking up at 6:00 a.m. on my birthday? Because I was almost 30, and that's what old people do. We wake up early.

I'd spent this past week pre-empting my family's birthday schemes. I needed to be so very clear.

"Do nothing," I'd told each of them every day since Monday. Mom reminded me this was my first birthday home since I was 18, which reminded me how far I was from 18.

"Stop saying you're almost 30 when you're 29, Lu," Gracie said yesterday when I told her for the fifth consecutive day to ignore my birthday. "I barely noticed when I turned 30 earlier this year."

"That's because you'd met all of your life goals by then."

"To be a hot, young mom?" she asked, shifting her weight on the stool. Her sigh filled the kitchen.

"To get married and be a mom," I clarified.

"Is that what you want?"

I shook my head and stood to clear our breakfast dishes, but Gracie put her hand on mine.

"Didn't you re-open Penny Thrift last week?" she asked.

"Yes."

"Successfully?"

"Not the pierogies."

"People ate plenty."

"Pity pierogies."

"And didn't you show me the revision of the church's anniversary book before you tucked me in last night?"

I nodded.

"And didn't I tell you when I came over this morning that it didn't put me to sleep like your first draft?"

"Okay, I get it," I said.

"Not to mention you're in the running for Aunt of the Year."

I smiled and squeezed Gracie's hand before taking the milk back to the fridge and the cereal to the pantry. I leaned against the cupboard instead of returning to my seat next to her.

"How things are and how they feel don't always sync, Gracie. Penny Thrift, the anniversary book — they're big. I'm grateful. But …"

I let the word hang in the air, not knowing how to fill the space behind it. Gracie looked at me, and then she looked away. I wondered if we were remembering the same thing — that morning after she was released from the hospital, and how her thankfulness and that gnawing feeling of "more" had co-existed. I hadn't thrown a one-liner at her then. She let this space alone, too and stood to go home.

"As your friend, I promise not to mention the 2-9 — which is not a 3-0 — tomorrow, but because I'm your friend I've also arranged for the girls to be somewhere else. No babysitting on the big day."

The quiet that greeted me when I got out of bed was the quiet I would have all day. I opened my bedroom door to a surprise — a vase of pink carnations from my dad. I sat them next to the cactus Jackson had given me after visiting his sister in Arizona last fall. I touched my finger to one of the spines. The succulent was Lu hardy. It had survived my New York sojourn, and I'd watered it once since I'd been back. The thing refused to die. I should throw it away, but I put the vase of flowers in front of it instead. Birthdays were not for making important decisions.

But the birthday surprises kept coming — the biggest surprise being their stealthy delivery. In the kitchen was a basket of buttermilk spice muffins sitting next to a full French press of coffee. While I dug into both, a text came in from Virginia to stay home from Penny Thrift and "do something fun."

Then Ted came through the back door with two cans of paint.

"Happy birthday, Lu-ser. How about I help you paint your rooms before I head into work?"

"How did you know which color to get?" I asked as we opened the door into the rooms. I hadn't moved past painting swatches on the walls – eight in the sitting room and five in the bedroom. Ted laughed and arranged the tarps and other painting supplies from the box Dad had lent me earlier in the week.

"Gracie told me which one you were leaning toward, and I went one lighter on the swatch."

"It looks white, Ted. I don't want this place to read asylum."

"It's not white, it's light, and it will make the rooms look bigger." He handed me a roller before taking a brush out of his back pocket. "I'll trim along the ceiling and molding. You follow with this."

I loved the color with his first stroke – white but with enough blue not to classify it as either. It was like the sky on a day you wouldn't notice the sky, and it gave the room breathing space – the color equivalent of opening the windows.

Ted painted like a professional, fast and confident with a touch of judgment.

"The goal is to get paint on the whole roller, not half," he said.

I dipped again.

"Then you make an M."

I did.

"Now fill it in to make a box."

I made a box.

"Lightly, Lu! You don't need to grind the paint into the wall."

"Maybe I like that look."

"Like you threw grits at the wall?"

"Like a beach."

"You can't take instruction."

"I shouldn't have to on my birthday, Ted. Pay attention to your own painting, or I'm going to catch up."

It was an empty boast, but Ted shut up, and I was too intent on my M's and squares to make conversation. My nerves eased up after the second wall, and by the time we were on the last, I decided painting was therapeutic. And fumey. I opened the doors leading to the deck, closing my eyes against the morning sun, the warm breeze offering a suggestion for what to do with my afternoon.

"I think I'll go to the creek after we're done," I shared with Ted. The height of his eyebrows told me he wasn't impressed.

"It's a fine way to spend a day," I defended.

"Sure, and maybe you'll catch some crawdads, too."

"Quit."

I turned back to the deck and leaned against the doorframe.

"Why not go on a date?"

I looked back at him. It was my turn to raise my eyebrows. "You're changing your tune."

"How?"

"Roddy told me what you told him in high school."

I'd hoped to make him feel guilty, but Ted started laughing. "You're your own man-repellant."

"Do you remember what Gracie said about being nice to me on my birthday?"

"All I'm saying is you're not the most approachable person. If I'd known what a bang-up job you'd do on your own, I would have toned down my locker room warning."

I crossed my arms over my chest. "What locker room warning?"

"Once in high school, a guy said something about you when he thought I wasn't listening."

"And?"

"I was listening. I shoved his face in the locker. He got stitches, and I had to sit out the next two games."

I kept looking at him. I knew there was more.

"I might have also reminded the team about the hands-off policy at the start of every season. That's all."

"This explains everything ever."

"Don't blame this all on me. You spent the majority of high school talking only to Gracie."

"Then how do you explain that I started dating John the minute I left?"

"You didn't start dating him until after you graduated college, but if I'd been around …"

"What?"

"I would have shoved his face into a locker."

I rolled my eyes. "I have no idea why Gracie married you."

"I don't talk to her like this."

"How do you … no. I don't want to know. Let's finish so I can get to the part of my birthday that doesn't involve you."

My words must have pricked a tiny, uncharted region of Ted's stone heart. He wrapped an arm around my shoulders after I picked up the roller.

"I'm messing with you, Lu. I threatened the team for a reason. I'll bet you ten bucks if you smiled at three random guys this week, you'd land a date. The problem is you aren't interested in random guys, and the one you are interested in ..."

He paused, looking at me with eyes the same brown as mine. Behind the color I saw a hesitancy I also recognized. Ted excelled at his role of pesky older brother, but he kept the heckling surface-level. He would drop what he was about to say if I asked him to, but I stood there, waiting.

"The one you are interested in isn't offering," he finished.

"So, what do I do?"

"Stand by the decision you made when you left and be done with it."

"Or?"

"Put up a fight, like you do with everyone else."

We finished the first coat by lunchtime. Ted headed home for his. I packed mine and changed into paint-free cut-offs to go to the creek.

When I was little and my dad was in charge of me for an afternoon, he'd turn the truck to the creek – not to the public access parking lot, but a couple miles down to an open field with a gravel drive and barn my dad had built for a client. I could still park there, my dad had assured me before I left.

I walked the invisible path through the tall grass, skimming my hands along its tips until the sound of the creek turned to sight. I slipped off my shoes and stepped in the water. The creek didn't know it was June, and the shock of the cold almost sidelined me to the bank with the book in my back pocket. I stepped forward instead, and by the time I waded shin-high, the cold of the creek and the warmth of the sun reached an understanding. I could now explore without registering the temperature of either.

I sifted my fingers along the creek bed for stones, having a vague idea I'd put some in a jar as decoration for my new rooms. I took my time, holding each to the sun like a curator. After collecting two-pockets worth, I stopped. The sun reflected off the surface of the water like glitter. Wading through it was an extravagance – a birthday fit for a princess.

I picked my way along until I found a slab of limestone large enough to sunbathe my finds and me. I laid out the stones in straight rows before settling next to them. I had nowhere to be. I leaned back on my hands, closed my eyes, and twinkled my toes against the current, listening to the sound of the creek meandering to who knows where.

Life was good. An objective fact, and I nodded as if someone had said it out loud. It was full with everything Gracie had detailed yesterday: good people and good work. The work busied my days and kept me out of my head, but it wasn't enough. Some of it was temporary. Gracie was due any day, and though she'd have a new baby, she'd be back to a more active role than she'd been on bed rest. I was one edit from finishing the anniversary book. Penny Thrift was part-mine in name, but Virginia's in every aspect that mattered. It fit with her dreams, her skills. She was made to run it.

And me?

How long had I pretended this question didn't exist, only for it to rise again and again? I was tired of swallowing it.

What about me?

I had so many questions, but I didn't feel I could ask them anymore than I could ask the question that pounded on repeat whenever I saw Jackson.

Do you see me?

I asked it out loud now and for the first time, I saw a path – the one I could have claimed if I'd made a different choice the morning I returned.

I could have driven to Jackson's house instead of mine. I could have spoken without hesitating.

Before I left, you asked me whether I believed God could save me. I didn't because I didn't think I needed to be saved. I do now.

Last night I saw a choice, to pretend I am whole or see I am broken. A broken person can't put herself back together. I saw I was that person. Then I saw Jesus, and I knew – I knew – I didn't have to stay broken. He could piece me whole.

I could have been honest.

I messed up with you, Jackson. I shut you out, and I'm sorry. I understand if you're angry with me. I don't blame you for moving on with someone else, and I won't stand in the way. But before I let you go, I need to know one thing.

Will you be with me?

I could have asked. I stretched out on the rock, extending my arms past my head to catch the creek with my hands. The minutes ran with the water, both flowing forward as my mind made sense of what happened from my last night in New York to now.

Being here was more than a chance. It was more than a new me in life as usual. It was new life. God hadn't called me back here to walk through another's plans. He hadn't called me daughter and raised me to stand in another woman's shadow.

The choice I had then was still mine now.

I sat up, and reached forward to cup the water with my hands. Most dripped away, but my skin jumped against the cool remainder that made it to my face. I stood, loaded the sunbaked stones back in my pockets and headed upstream.

CHAPTER 37: JACKSON

She was eating cake when we got there. The way Louisa eats cake –
frosting only. She did it without thought, so tuned into the ritual that
she didn't see us coming up the driveway. She scraped the frosting
off the top, moved to the back and then knocked off the top layer to
scrape the middle.

Her fork paused, and I could tell she was debating whether to eat
the actual cake, but she set it down at Roddy's happy birthday shout.
I didn't know today was her birthday. He did and had driven us here,
before I could weigh the idea. Of course, it's always a good idea to
wish someone a happy birthday, but this was Louisa eating cake on a
summer night and wearing cut-offs and a tank top. It brought my
mind to last summer.

I needed to leave. I hadn't followed Roddy off the driveway to the
deck. Louisa's body turned to him as he hugged her, but her brown
eyes were on me.

Ten minutes, and I'd find a way to go.

Then Roddy took out his phone.

"Shit, Lu. I'm sorry. I've got to go deal with something."

"Like what?" She put her hands on her hips. We both knew what
Roddy was doing, and I should have come to her – to our – defense
to call him out, but my eyes wouldn't move from her hips.

"Work."

"On a Saturday night?"

I moved my eyes in time to see Roddy smile at her, wrap his arm
around her waist, and kiss her cheek. He's never been subtle. He
looked at me and smiled.

"You coming, Jack?"

I looked at Louisa, looking so much like she had last summer. I hadn't wished her happy birthday yet. From the color on her face, I could tell she'd spent part of it outside. I wanted her to tell me about it.

I wasn't going anywhere.

"I'll stay."

"How will you get home?" Roddy asked.

I looked at him, punching him in the face with my eyes. "I'll figure it out."

He left, whistling as he walked down the driveway. I heard Louisa laugh and my eyes followed the sound. Now that I'd made my choice, I couldn't stay on the driveway and look at her standing barefoot in the grass. I smiled and stepped forward.

"I have two words for you, birthday girl."

She tilted her head to the side and smiled back. "And what are those, Jackson?"

"Corn hole."

"Isn't that one word?"

We decided to settle it with a game, and I pulled the boards from under the deck. She brought the bags from the garage, telling me about her day at the creek like we were picking up a conversation from yesterday, instead of the polite ones we'd had since she'd been back. I'd missed how she tells things – how it puts me where she's been. It made me wish I'd been there. Within minutes, she was emptying her pockets to show me the stones she'd collected. She insisted each carried unique qualities. I'm sure they did, but I couldn't see them. She rolled her eyes at my underwhelmed reaction, and I laughed.

"You don't need my permission to put your little rocks in a jar."

"Every word in your sentence is dismissive, J."

She pocketed all but two of her rocks. "Let me break it down for you. This is a rectangle, and this is a circle."

"How did I not see that before?"

"Now come closer."

I stepped forward. No hesitation where there should have been. I could smell the sun on her skin.

"What color do you see?" she asked.

"Gray."

"And?"

"Gray."

Louisa handed me a rock, closing my fingers around it. "It's a dove gray, and if you rub your thumb along the surface, you'll feel it's as smooth as it looks. Now look at this one."

She turned her back to me and held up the second rock to the light from the deck. My eyes followed the path from her shoulder to her hand. A slight turn of her hand, and my eyes caught a different light. She did it again, and there were more coming from the rock.

She put her hand down and turned to me. "Do you see?"

I saw her. I saw her other hand in front of me, palm up. I reached mine forward, registering at the last second she was holding it out to re-claim her rock. She set both on the deck rail.

"Consider this the spoils pot. You'd better get your head in the game."

The best suggestion of the night. Louisa landed her first throw in the hole.

"You've been practicing," I said.

"What else do I have to do with my time?"

She'd said it sarcastically, and I paused instead of throwing my bag. "You selling yourself short?"

"Maybe." Then she shook her head and sighed. "Wait, no. I am. I am selling myself short, and I told myself I wouldn't do that anymore."

"I will pray for you," I responded, and she threw a bag at me, which I caught and tossed into the hole.

"I'm claiming those points," she said.

"You're going to need them," I said before landing my own bag.

"You ready for the church anniversary?"

I must have asked her about a dozen times since she'd been back. It was a safe question with a safe answer. I didn't blame Louisa for ignoring it now.

"I'd rather talk about what you're preaching on."

"Abraham's sacrifice of Isaac. What about it?"

She laughed. "You're so steeped in this stuff it reads like normal to you, but Genesis is like a bad soap opera. How many times is Abraham going to pretend Sarah is his sister?"

"What, you've never made the same mistake twice? If the stories in the Bible were easy to read, they wouldn't be honest. God deals with real people."

"So that's the point – to see we're made of the same ingredients?"

"For me, it's more of a starting point to see God's grace – not just to save people like Abraham and me, but to use us. Anything He might ask in return seems small in comparison."

"In this case, Abraham killing his son."

"In this case, a test. Who is more important to Abraham, God or Isaac? God knew the answer, but Abraham needed to know it for himself. His love for his son was holding him back."

We'd crossed the yard, and it was Louisa's turn, but she stared at the bags in her hands. I put mine down and turned to her.

"What is it?"

She took her time before answering.

"It's a story about letting go," she said.

"Not all the time. God asks us to fight, too, but never for the things that stand in between us and him." She didn't say anything, but there was more. I gave her a minute before asking her the question she was asking herself. "Do you think He's asking you to give something up?"

"I don't know," she said. "The natural choice seems to put up a fight – at least that's what everyone keeps telling me."

She turned away to face the board across the yard. The breeze caught her hair, but she didn't notice. She didn't notice me looking at her. Louisa had often felt like two people to me – the girl who did everything she could to go unnoticed and the girl who, once she let you in, kept you there. The truth of her wasn't she was two, but there was a lot to the one – so much to this one woman.

I was still staring at her when she looked at me, one hand still holding the corn hole bag and the other brushing her hair back from her face.

"Maybe the real fight, Jackson, is letting go."

Louisa turned and threw her bag to start the next round. The sound of the bag landing on the board cut whatever it was I'd been feeling since I'd seen her from the driveway. I took a breath and focused on losing the game as quickly as possible to get out of her backyard before I did something I'd need to apologize for.

"Best of three?" Louisa asked when she had won.

"I have to go."

She nodded. "No late nights before Sunday preaching. I get it."

She didn't get it at all, but she tossed me her keys instead of offering to drive me home.

"Take my car and leave the keys on the front seat. I'll get it from your place after church tomorrow."

"Abraham's sacrifice of Isaac is big – a Top 10 Bible moment. We refer to it so often I think we forget what's happening here. God is telling Abraham to kill his son."

I looked up from my notes – the ones I'd written after I left Louisa's house.

"Our sacrifices are different, but we all have them. Each one of us has something standing in the way of seeing God as He is. For Abraham, it was Isaac. The child through which God would bless the nations had become Abraham's everything. God is calling him to make a clean break in this chapter.

"Was this the first and only time God had asked Abraham to lay this idol down? We don't know, but I think it's important to note some of our sacrifices are a repeated offering because try as we might the first, second, or twentieth time, we can't seem to take our hands off."

I looked at her. I should have looked around. But what I had to say was for Louisa and me.

"I know for myself, it's the desire to do right. I was a slave to this when I was younger, careful to keep in line. I wanted to live my life above others' criticism. My divorce cured me of the idea I could somehow live a life so perfect it canceled the need for a savior. Lately, I find myself in the same pattern. My need to do right – to continue the decisions I've made with good intention – has stopped me from seeing, believing, in God's power to resurrect. To redeem. To make new."

I didn't talk to Louisa after church, and her car was gone from my driveway by the time I got home. On my porch rail, she'd left the two rocks, a slice of birthday cake, and a note.

"Try not to swallow it whole."

CHAPTER 38: LU

Air thick enough to swim through and mass humanity screaming on what they paid to ride – there wasn't one thing I liked about Dunlap Days, including the name. Years of failed school levies back in the 1970s made the district desperate, and someone on the PTA brainstormed rides bolted to the ground as the solution. Though the levy crisis had passed, Dunlap Days remained and continued to raise heaps of cash.

"It paid for Caroline's class trip to the aquarium this year," Gracie said in her fevered pitch to get me to chaperone. The final proof for the anniversary book was to the printer, and I'd just set my butt in a chair with a book to celebrate when Gracie appeared with bribery hot chocolate that was slightly steamier than the outdoors. I drank it anyway.

"Lu, I'm desperate. The babysitter who was supposed to take them canceled, your mom is helping Nana pack, and your dad and Ted are stuck at work."

"Why can't we lean on small town kindness and drop the girls off?" I joked. "Someone will take care of them."

"Because that's wrong. Also, Caroline is the only one tall enough to go on the rides by herself." She handed me a baggy of oyster crackers. "You're going to need these."

I scoffed. "I have a stomach of steel."

"When was the last time you tested that?"

"High school. Gravitron."

"Things change. Ted will relieve you after he gets off work."

I checked out her belly, but there was no amusement park workaround for a lady who was nine months pregnant and supposed to be on bed rest.

"I'll get the girls ready," Gracie said.

I drank, stringing out the hot chocolate as I formed a Plan B. It started with sitting my nieces at the kitchen table with popsicles. They obliged, their ponytails bouncing as their legs scissored back and forth.

"How about we go see a movie instead of Dunlap Days?"

"No," they chirped in unison.

"A sleepover in Aunt Lu's room?"

"We've already done that," Caroline said.

"Haven't you already 'done' Dunlap Days?"

"Not since last summer," Abigail said, "and I can go on more rides now because I'm taller."

"Barely. You're seven."

"How old are you, Aunt Lu?" Holly asked.

"She's almost 30," Caroline said.

"Twenty-nine," I corrected, but it got me nowhere.

To Dunlap Days we went. The heat from the asphalt met the heat from the sun at the center of my brain, making me delirious by the end of the first hour. When the girls suggested ice cream, I led the charge, though it was ten in the morning.

They downed their cones and ran to the next ride – airplanes trolling in a tame circle that I was two-feet too tall for. I settled on the nearest bench, contemplating my age-old struggle of woman versus ice cream cone on a hot day. As always, I thought about it too long, and by the time the girls' flight took off, the ice cream had melted everywhere.

I heard Jackson's laugh before I saw him. "Now where have I seen this before?"

He reached into his back pocket and produced a handkerchief. I didn't know men under 65 carried those.

I grimaced. "Is that used?"

"Does it matter?"

I took it. Jackson handed me a water bottle for what turned into a Dunlap Days' sponge bath that reached to my ankles. Where hadn't the ice cream dripped?

I handed him the hankie, but Jackson stepped back.

"Keep it."

I pocketed it and scanned around him. There was no sign of Rebecca. My adult family members were also absent, and the nieces were too high with thrill-ride hysteria and sugar to require my attention beyond height regulations. It made for odd circumstances to feel alone with Jackson, but I did.

"Where's Rebecca?" I asked, just to make sure.

"She's helping her parents with something and won't be back until later tonight. I'm making my rounds as quickly as possible before heading home. It's been a long week."

He turned away as he said it, but I used the Tilt-A-Whirl as an excuse to keep him.

"I might puke if I have to do that with them," I said.

He looked at me, ready to object, but he was immune to the girls, who dragged him along to this ride and the next five. He convinced me to join on the last one – a ferris wheel with enclosed cars that turned upside down. I didn't puke, but I took to the bench next to the pavilion to practice deep breathing techniques. I remembered the oyster crackers and munched them one at a time. Jackson took his time laughing at me, breaking to chomp into the cotton candy my nieces handed him when they bee-lined it to the dance floor.

"I bet your nana could hold her stomach better than you."

"If you'd call her in to relieve me, I'd appreciate it. Ted should have been here a half hour ago."

The girls rushed over, grabbing Jackson for a dance. I finished the baggie and walked over to watch, catching some interesting choreography to the tail-end of "Sweet Home Alabama," a musical staple at this thing. The band switched to something slower, and the girls changed modes, leaving Jackson behind so they could twirl in solo circles.

He walked over to me, and I supposed we could have stood there, watching them, but my right hand moved without permission, touching his arm in the same way as it had my first morning back. Jackson gave me a different look this time.

"Dance with me?" I asked.

A second passed. And another. His eyes scanned the crowd for the third and fourth. By the fifth I was sure he'd say, "No," but he took my hand and stepped onto the dance floor. His other hand found my waist.

"You stepped on my toe," Jackson said.

"I didn't say I could dance. I asked if you would."

He stopped moving, and my second of bravery vanished. This was a bad idea, and I stepped back to pull away. Jackson held me fast.

"I'm sorry for my part in what happened between us last year, Louisa. Coming around so much and asking you to stay before you left for New York. I had no right to do those things when we weren't …"

"Don't apologize, Jackson. I knew what I was doing."

"I apologized for what I was doing."

"Don't do that." My lungs needed air.

"But I was wrong to …"

"Be my friend?"

He stepped back, looking at me.

"I wasn't your friend," he said.

"And I wasn't yours."

"Which is why I'm apologizing."

"No." I stepped back, but I kept my eyes on his. "Isn't it enough it took you only a couple months to move past me? Isn't it enough I stand on the sidelines, unable to do the same? Now is what it is, Jackson, but don't apologize to me for before. Right or wrong, I wish it back all the time. You have no idea how much I'd give to have your attention again."

There they were – the words I'd taken so long to find. They took less than a minute to say.

"You left," he said.

"I left."

"I asked you to stay."

"But not with you."

"Would that have made a difference?"

"I don't know, but my leaving didn't change anything for me."

"Which was what?"

"I was yours."

He shook his head as if to toss aside what I'd said.

"You left to be with John. That's an odd way of showing you wanted to be with me."

"I was with him, and I know it doesn't make sense, but it doesn't change, it never changed …"

I hesitated.

"It didn't change what, Louisa?"

I knew what I needed to say, but I took a moment first.

"I was yours when I left and yours when I came back. It was you who didn't wait for me."

This wasn't the place to stand still — the loud band, the twirling nieces, the people everywhere, but neither of us moved. For the first time since I'd been back, I'd left nothing unsaid. And I had nothing else to say. The next move was Jackson's, and I intended to stay right here until he turned away or spoke.

But my phone buzzed in my pocket. I would have ignored it, but Caroline stopped her twirling and shrieked. She took a phone from her pocket — the one Ted had given her for one purpose.

It was baby time.

CHAPTER 39: JACKSON

I left the dance floor in a trance. I broke up with Rebecca in a trance.

When I think of what it took for Louisa and me to get here, the conversation with Rebecca was unbelievably direct. She knew from how I said hello that I had more to say, and instead of inviting me into her place, she stepped onto the porch and closed the door behind her, leaning against it as she waited for me to start.

"Something's happened."

"It's Lu, right?" she asked. "We talked about this right after she came back and then again at my place. I gave you an out both times."

I remembered. "I was honest with you."

"But not with yourself." She looked down before looking back at me. "Are you going to be with her now?"

"I don't know."

It was a bad answer to her brave question, but it was honest – something I hadn't been for a long time, as Rebecca had pointed out.

"I'm sorry, Rebecca. Looking back, I can see how this has been coming for a while, but it wasn't as clear in the middle of it. You have been nothing but wonderful, and I wish …"

She stepped forward.

"You wish what, Jackson?"

"That you weren't in the middle of it."

"Which is a different wish than being with me."

I nodded, and she stepped back, turned and closed the door.

I left her front porch in a trance and came here in a trance – not the old church, but the new one where I'd preached every Sunday since Louisa came back. I sat beside the pulpit and stared at where she always sat. I didn't need her here to see her.

When had I exchanged honesty for righteousness or at least the appearance of it? I wanted to be right so badly – to live right, to do what was right. But the more I'd tried to pursue that with Louisa, to have the "right" conversations, to stay away, the farther I was from it. My apology was supposed to be a cut off, but Louisa had walked through it like a door.

I leaned my elbows on my knees and rubbed my hands along my face before folding them. I sought God, grateful for the muscle memory my own father had taught me from before I could remember. First, we praise God for all He is. Then, we praise God for all He has done. Next, we confess.

Then – then – we ask. We ask for what we want. Even now, with her words clearing the way, I hesitated. The words for what I wanted felt impossible, but true. True was true, and there was no point in any of this if I didn't say it out loud.

"I want to be with her."

The words filled the sanctuary, sustaining me for the wait.

"Can I be with her?"

CHAPTER 40: LU

I brought the girls to the waiting room in record time, and everyone looked ready to settle in. Nana Bea sat next to the front window with a gardening magazine. Mom and Dad were already nose-deep in books, and I was set to join them after I popped into the delivery room to let Gracie know I was here.

She looked great, and I matched her smile of relief with one of my own. Making it this far was a shared accomplishment. I gave her a quick hug.

"Congratulations, Gracie. I'll bring in the girls when the baby comes."

She gripped my right hand when I tried to move to the door. I looked at Ted, who was manning her left flank. His smile tipped me that I was in for it.

"You're staying, Lu," Gracie said.

No was my first thought. *Gross*, my second.

"The girls …"

"Ted brought electronic babysitters, and your parents can take care of their vending machine demands."

"Isn't this supposed to be a private thing?"

"That was making the baby. Haven't you noticed all the people in and out of here?"

True. In our brief interchange, two people in scrubs had come in. The doctor I'd sort of yelled at when Gracie was here a couple months ago was in the room. We were doing a good job avoiding eye contact.

"But I don't know what to do," I said, trying to yank my hand back.

"That's what these other people are for."

"Why does it take so many people to get a baby out? I thought that was your job."

"They're here to tell us what the beeps on the machines mean. Stop stalling and settle in," Gracie ordered before her breathing changed — faster, urgent. I held mine because I wasn't sure if there was enough oxygen in the room for Gracie, Ted, me, and the hospital staff. Another person came in.

"I don't know if I want to be in here," I whispered to Gracie.

"You don't get a vote, Lu!" Her shout was for me, but I wasn't sure about the subsequent scream. I looked at Ted.

"Contraction."

Oh.

"And don't grip her hand," he instructed.

"But she's gripping mine. I thought it'd be a show of solidarity."

"Only she's allowed to do the gripping."

I looked at Gracie to confirm, but then Ted said, "Don't look at her while she's in the middle of a contraction."

"How do you know all of this?"

He raised three fingers, which did make him the in-house expert. Suddenly, Gracie released her grip and stopped screaming.

"Now you can look at her and make small talk," Ted said, looking at his watch before adding another time to a running list on a yellow legal pad. "You have 5 minutes, give or take 20 seconds, before the next one."

I looked at the bed.

"She's fine with you sitting on the bed between contractions."

"Shut up, Ted," Gracie said before yanking me onto the bed next to her. "I don't know why he thinks he needs to play cruise director."

Ted's eye roll said something about that, but he kept a lid on it.

"Your job is to fill in the downtimes with interesting stories," Gracie told me. "Go."

"I told Jackson I liked him," I said, leading with the night's headline.

"It's not news you like Jackson, Lu," Ted interrupted, in a voice a little too loud. "I bet the nurses know that."

"They do now!" I shouted at him.

Gracie, now back to herself and remembering her other major role in life, mediated.

"Ted, please pretend you're not in the room." She looked back at me and smiled. "You didn't use those words, right? 'I like you, Jackson.'"

"No, but I did tell him at Dunlap Days, so that whole middle school vibe was in play."

"Weren't you supposed to be watching the girls?"

"I blame the girls. They were the reason we were on the dance floor."

"A dance floor?" Tears filled her eyes. "That's so romantic."

Ted and I started laughing at the same time.

"What?"

I nodded to Ted. He could take this one.

"Look around the room, honey. Do you see Jackson?" he asked.

She looked at me. "Is he in the waiting room?"

I shook my head.

"Do you need to cry?" she asked, ugly crying enough for the both of us. "I'm worried you're not crying."

"I'm a little preoccupied."

Another contraction queued, supplanting Gracie's crying with screaming for the next 47 seconds, according to Ted's chart. I did a much better job obeying the operating instructions this round, and after a couple more, I settled into the groove of pretending like Gracie wasn't here when she was in contraction and entertaining her with stories when she wasn't. The topics shifted, but she managed to find something to cry about with each one. Three times, she tried to get me to call Jackson. One time, she tried to hook me up with the doctor. And right before things got hairy with non-stop contractions, she berated me for not bringing her cotton candy. I guess she was only allowed to have ice chips in here.

Labor is a beautiful, disgusting thing. I resolved never to witness another while simultaneously feeling like I'd missed out by not seeing the previous three. It was a flurry of activity focused around one purpose and impossible for me to track who came and went and what they did. The roles shifted with the moment and toward the end those moments blinked by. Here was Gracie, focused and in pain, but silent now. There was Ted, calm and ready. He was the first to hold his baby girl. I didn't hear her cry, but I saw his tears. Birth is messy, the baby was messy, but Ted cradled her to his chest anyway, touching his forehead to hers before placing her on Gracie. Ted and Gracie smiled at each other, a moment that proved her wrong. This was private. I was honored they'd invited me in.

Finally, there was me, holding baby Anabel by the window because Gracie said she needed natural light. Gracie also wanted to be cleaned up before the girls came in, and she wanted pizza. Ted left to get both while the nurses helped Gracie change and move her to a new bed. It was quiet long before I noticed.

Gracie's eyes were closed, and I couldn't tell if she was sleeping. I looked from her to the baby, wondering who Anabel would take after. Her face was too scrunched to tell her nose from her cheeks, and she was so small. Holding her was like a nothing.

"I'm glad I was here." I didn't expect an answer. I just wanted to say it out loud.

"In the room or in town?" Gracie asked a few seconds later.

"Both."

"Remember how angry I was when you left for New York?"

The pit from that memory settled in my chest. I opened my mouth to apologize again. Gracie beat me to it.

"I'm sorry I reacted like that, Lu. You deserved better from me."

"Why would you apologize to me? I was the one who did something wrong."

"Because you don't see yourself." She opened her eyes and turned her head to smile at Anabel and me. "I know you've felt lost. I know you feel like things happen to you, and maybe they do, but Lu … don't you see how you flip them around? Since you've been back, you have picked up every piece of my life, without complaint. Last year, I accused you of making the rest of us pick up your pieces. I pointed the finger, and I'm sorry."

I looked from Gracie to Anabel. I remembered Gracie crying when she found out she was having another girl, and I smiled. *Being a girl is hard work,* I silently whispered to Anabel. *There will be a lot of people who will tell you what you should do, so you're going to need to know what you want. You're going to have to go after it. And sometimes it takes a few times until you get it right.*

I would be here to help her, but I'd stand a much better chance of doing it if I saw my next decision through.

I turned to Gracie.

"Seeing you, seeing her, makes me feel brave. I have something I want to share with you, and I want you to hear me out before you say anything."

Of course, Gracie didn't like my plan, at least not the first part, but she let me talk, her face expressionless.

"This is important to you," she said after I'd finished. Whether she said it as a statement or a question, I wasn't sure.

"This is important to me."

Our moment was almost up. I heard my nieces screeching down the hallway before I spied them from the windows. Mom, Dad, and Nana followed close behind with Ted bringing up the rear and holding two boxes from Creek's. I handed Anabel to Gracie as they barged in. The girls' requests to eat pizza, kiss their mom, and hold their baby sister filled the air. It was enough to drive out everything we'd said, but Gracie was a pro.

"You have three days," she told me over the crowd.

I smiled. I needed to make one quick stop at home, and then I'd be in the car and on my way.

CHAPTER 41: JACKSON

I went to her house and then to Ted's. Both were dark and locked. Of course, Gracie having a baby would be a group effort, this was Louisa's family after all, and I kicked myself for wasting time.

People shouldn't drive this fast, I thought as I gunned the engine after coasting through a stop sign. It would buy me a second, but I couldn't get past the feeling it was a second I needed. I parked in the handicapped spot at the hospital. The people working the welcome desk saw me do it, but church business brought me here a lot. They knew who I was.

"I will move my car in 5 minutes," I told them, not breaking my stride.

No need to ask for Gracie's room number. I could hear her family from the stairwell door.

They stopped talking when I came in the room. I didn't cut the quiet with a hello. I scanned the room and then again to make sure. Louisa wasn't here.

I looked at Gracie. I should congratulate her.

"Where is she?" I asked instead.

Gracie has a great smile. It took over the room now.

"New York."

CHAPTER 42: LU

The bag was heavy. One knock would open the door, and I could walk across the apartment to set it on the kitchen counter before the bottom gave out. But I hesitated in front of his door now, like I'd hesitated yesterday with my phone in my hand.

My resolution and doubt revolved and tumbled as I had navigated to his number in the slowest way possible, ignoring the favorites and the search for a lazy scroll through the alphabet. This bought me ten seconds. I tapped the name, and his picture appeared, the one I'd taken of him drinking coffee at the kitchen island this past winter. His head was turned to the window, and the stillness of the profile captured him but hid his face.

My text was simple. I was in town and did he want to have dinner? I wasn't sure if he'd answer or how he'd answer. When I left New York, we'd agreed for him to go his way and me to go mine, and we hadn't been in touch since.

But John's answer was immediate. *Yes.*

"You look different," I blurted when I knocked, and he opened the door.

He looked better. His hair, normally kept under tight regulation with a weekly trip to the barber, was longer – not enough to classify as long to other people, but I knew. He'd grown a beard where at the most there'd been Sunday scruff. He was wearing glasses. Top collar unbuttoned and sleeves rolled to the elbows. No watch. Blue eyes, clear and sharp. Who knows how long I would have tallied the details if his smile hadn't cut me off.

"You look great," John said, stepping aside for me and my grocery bag like this was a normal thing. I cut through the living area to the kitchen without pause, my quick scan of the place not registering any significant changes. Still sparse, still bachelor. I set the bag on the counter and started emptying ingredients for chicken noodle soup.

John raised his eyebrows.

"You're cooking?" he asked, not trying to hide his surprise. I'd cooked one thing – pork and sauerkraut – in the six years we were together, and he'd hated it. "When you said you were going to bring something I'd never eaten before, I was skeptical."

"You're always skeptical," I responded, turning to him for a proper hello hug. For a count of three, I gave into the feel of him. Then, I stepped back. "Thank you for seeing me."

"Thank you for calling. Often as I think about you, I never pictured this." His eyes panned the island full of groceries, still not believing.

"You cook?" he asked again.

"Take a seat and prepare to be amazed. In the time it takes to chop this up, you can catch me up on your life."

I still didn't know whether I liked cooking, but right now, I liked that it gave me something to do while John talked. He kept the recap broad, talking about his new job and the cases he was working on. He caught me up on his family and a trip he'd just come back from. By the time I was finished dicing, he changed the course. I think we were both ready for it.

"I resigned from the firm the Monday after you left, and within the week, I couldn't understand why I'd stayed so long or why I ever wanted that life in the first place. Why did we move here after law school? Maybe if we'd stayed where we were I would have been more concerned about us instead of my job. Maybe we would still be together. I thought about that a lot after you left."

He leaned forward on his elbows. I pushed aside the cutting board to do the same, reaching my hands across the island to wrap around his.

We looked at each other for a long time. The silence wasn't uncomfortable – that's what history will do for you. The same went for the unchecked gaze. It was as if we needed the resolve in the other's eyes to settle the hypotheticals.

"I was one year too late in asking that question," John said.

"Probably two."

"Maybe three."

"But those first few years we were together …"

If I closed my eyes, I could see us then, but I hadn't come here to do that. John rewarded me with a smile for keeping them open. I released my hands and stood back. It was time to finish making soup, and I was glad I was facing the stockpot for what he said next.

"I'm seeing someone, Lu."

What was with these men? They moved on so fast. I shook my head, but I didn't say anything. I scraped the carrots, onions, and celery into the stockpot. I registered the smell as the vegetables hit the melted butter on the hot steel. I stirred, added salt, and stirred again. I took a sip of the water, buying a few more seconds of response time before I turned back to him.

"This is good news," I said.

The relief showed in his smile, followed by our first awkward moment of the night. I wasn't sure whether I could ask for more information, but it felt strange to talk about anything else.

"Do you want to know about her?"

"Dying to," I finished.

John smiled and spread his hands, sitting back. "What do you want to know?"

"Let's start with her name."

He'd met Ellie soon after I left – at church of all places. If there was any detail that could move me from curiosity about the new girl, John going to church was it.

"I didn't know what to do after you left. I moved from wandering around the apartment to wandering into the church you'd gone to. I walked in, hoping to find … I'm not sure. Maybe you hiding out?"

I laughed.

"I found Pastor Eddy, instead."

I laughed harder. "Eddy!"

"My law school professors have nothing on that man. He doesn't care he's preaching to lawyers, stockbrokers, trust fund babies, and everyone else who thinks they run this city."

"That's a good way to describe him. Did he get you to meet with him?"

"Within the week."

"And?"

He leaned forward. "You sound like Eddy."

"It's just a question."

"No, it's not."

He was right, but I maintained my wide-eyed innocence anyway. "Searching, but no answers yet."

He smiled when he said it, knowing he was repeating the words I'd given him for going to church after I came back to New York.

"You described it well, Lu. At that point, I had a lot of questions, but I'm not convinced they're questions with answers or ones that require answers. I didn't go to church more than a couple times, and I haven't felt the need to go back."

I wanted to counter, which took me by surprise, but maybe it shouldn't have. I'd talked about God with John more than anyone else.

"It's not a head game, John. It's not about being convinced, so much as it's … I don't know how to describe when acknowledging something as true with your mind moves to surrendering to that truth. My last night here, after I'd messed up with you – used you – that's what happened."

"Like a coping mechanism," he concluded. Sharp, this man. He could never have been anything but a lawyer. I shook my head.

"The opposite – like everything up until that moment was the coping mechanism and believing in God was the first true step."

"How has that turned out for you? You've done a great job of not talking about yourself since you walked through the door."

I filled the stockpot with broth to simmer before sitting next to him, our shoulders touching.

"Home is different. Not bad different, but awkward. Sometimes, I feel like I know who I am, and sometimes, I feel like I need to be someone else."

"Are you thinking of coming back here?"

I shook my head and kept shaking it when he asked the next one.

"The guy?"

"No to both. I came here because I'm thinking about starting something, and I needed to talk to my old boss, Molly, at *NYNY*."

"Couldn't you have picked up the phone?"

His rang as if on cue, and I saw Ellie's name and picture flash. I grabbed it from John's hand and looked at her picture as one ring turned to two and three. There hadn't been enough time since he'd told me about her to imagine what she looked like, but I would never have guessed. Cute with short hair that framed a fresh face that looked like it had never seen make-up. She didn't need it.

"Nose ring?" I silently mouthed as if she could hear us.

"Are you going to answer or should I?"

I tossed it back to him, and he hadn't finished his hello before her voice cut in – loud, no speakerphone needed.

"You aren't sleeping with your ex-girlfriend are you?"

"Lu turned me down."

"John, you bastard."

And then I didn't hear the rest because he walked to the living room. I gripped the island not to fall off my barstool. Who was this guy? John was many things, but in my experience, playful wasn't one of them. I couldn't help but lean back and track him as he wandered around the living room, alternating laughing with teasing his new girlfriend. I didn't bother to shift my focus when he turned around a few minutes later and caught me staring. How could I not?

My curiosity about Ellie filled the rest of our dinner conversation. She sounded great. John made her sound great. As he'd said, they'd met on one of the Sundays he'd gone to church after I left. Eddy brought her in because she headed a non-profit the church supported to bring classes about environmental sustainability to inner city schools.

"Yes, but how did you meet her?"

"I'd quit my job, and her pitch gave me something to do. I wrote a big check right there, took it up to her, and she asked me out to lunch. She told me later she'd asked because she hoped to get more money out of me." John laughed before he paused, his mind replaying a memory he wasn't going to share. "One lunch turned to another, and now Ellie drags me all over the city. You saved me tonight from having to go to an outdoor concert fundraiser. You know how I feel about sitting on grass."

Light – a word I never would have used to describe John – was the best word to put to him now. "You don't look like you mind."

He shrugged.

"She sounds great, John."

"I wish you could meet her."

"I've already made my chicken noodle soup for a boy and his girl this year. That's plenty."

"What if I took you both to dinner tomorrow?"

"Can't. Gracie gave me a time limit. I need to be back in Dunlap's Creek by tomorrow night."

"And if you aren't?"

"I turn into a pumpkin."

"Not possible."

I squeezed his hand. "Let me help clean up before I go."

It had been our shared, daily chore. John and I worked in quiet – more our speed than filling the space talking. It would have been hard for me to find words, anyway. I was too overwhelmed by a sense of timing, wondering why mine was off – months too late for Jackson and years too early for John. What if John and I had met now, when we had a better sense of who we were and how to offer that to another person?

I was glad to see he was doing well, but I hadn't come here just to check in. John put the stockpot away, and I dried my hands on the kitchen towel. We matched our steps, taking our time crossing the small apartment to the front door. I turned to him instead of reaching for the handle.

"I'm sorry for what I did, John."

He crossed his arms over his chest. "I have no regrets. Our second chance didn't end the way I wanted, but I think we tried."

"I hurt you."

It hurt to say it and something in how John looked down and shifted his weight told me the pain wasn't all gone.

"You did, but I'm okay."

All that was left now was to leave. Before John opened the front door, he lifted my chin with his hand, and in his eyes I saw a lot. All our shared stories, all we knew about each other. Anyone who came after would be at the mercy of replay – what we chose to share or to keep to ourselves. Whenever I'd thought about John in the last couple months, I saw that last night. But now, I saw our first night when he tried to kiss me. I saw all the nights we'd sat on the couch, dreaming about living in this city together. That hadn't worked out for us, but not because of any one reason or any one person. A relationship doesn't boil down to one moment, one wrong or one right. It's all of it, which I think is why I also saw grace in his eyes – the unmerited favor that comes from love. I didn't deserve John's forgiveness. He gave it because he loved me. It was the same love that had brought me back to him, to forgive him and try again. Our love had shifted, but it wasn't gone.

I closed my hand around his and smiled at him before stepping back. He opened the door.

"Goodbye, Lu."

"Goodbye, John."

CHAPTER 43: LU

It was one piece of paper and the most dramatic thing I'd packed. I could have thrown it away at home. I'd told myself that as I laid it on top of the clothes I'd packed before I left Dunlap's Creek. I zipped it in my duffle bag instead. I would throw the paper away, but there was a natural order to these things, and it began with a bench.

If it weren't for Ted, I'd never have noticed this place. I'd run away to New York last winter, but searched for home all over the city. The stained glass of a church near John's apartment reminded me of the designs Ted had carved into the wood pillars of the new church back home. I'd crossed through the wrought iron gate to take a picture and noticed the bench in the middle of the small surrounding garden. I didn't sit on the bench that day, but I did the next day – and the next and the next. Sitting on the bench outside the church turned to sitting in a pew inside the church and hearing the words of the Bible in a different way.

This paper started all of that. I don't remember why Jackson had written the first part of Ecclesiastes 3 for me last summer, but it held me then as it did now. How many times had I folded and unfolded this paper? How many places had I carried it in my back pocket?

It had the consistency of soft pulp. I fingered the edges on my lap, closed my eyes and whispered the verses from memory, not knowing I could until now. *There is a time for everything, and a season for every activity under heaven.* Indifference didn't accompany my recitation; the words still stirred me.

What time is it now?

My question was a prayer, and on this bench, holding this paper, I was ready to hear the answer. I'd claimed to return home without expectation, but that wasn't true. I'd hoped God would bring Jackson back to me, but the man who'd written Ecclesiastes 3 on this paper wasn't the Jackson I knew now. He didn't see me. I don't think he remembered the time when he had, and I needed to stop waiting around like that was going to change.

I breathed out. It wasn't what I wanted. It just was. The next step was obvious. Throw the paper away; let the man go. I didn't want to do this. I wanted to want to do this. That's two degrees from perfection, but it was a start.

Leave it to Pastor Eddy to walk through the gate at the point I was ready to stand. The last time I saw him was my last Sunday here, but he didn't seem surprised to see me any more than he seemed concerned that church began in an hour. He set his bag down and sat next to me.

"I meant to email you," I said.

"What would your email have said?"

"I believe in God and am heading back home." I smiled over how easily the words came.

"How have things been going?"

"I've had good days and bad days."

"What have you been reading in the Bible?"

"Abraham."

"Then you know there's going to be a lot more of all that. Are you staying for church?"

"Yes, but I'd like to ask you something," I said, standing and folding the paper to put in my back pocket. I unfolded it again, holding it with both hands like a brace for what I was about to say.

"Would you baptize me first?" I knew churches had a protocol for these things, but I held my breath like it was now or never.

He gave a swift nod and walked to the double wooden doors of the church. "Sure. Make sure you throw out that paper on the way in."

I stared at his back with all the surprise in the world, and then Eddy threw me another. He smiled.

"I'm not a prophet, Lu. I've done this just long enough to know what a girl crying over a piece of paper on a bench means."

I laughed. "I must seem ridiculous."

He stopped messing with the lock on the front door and turned to me.

"No. I think you understand whatever is on that paper, whatever it means to you, you need to let it go before you come inside. It doesn't mean you walk through these doors without doubt, but it does mean you're making a choice. Everything God asks of us comes to that – distinct choices to live for God or something else."

Eddy popped the lock and used both arms to open the doors wide. There was no break between the entry and sanctuary, and without the interior lights turned on, the stained glass windows took the show.

"I'm ready when you are," he said before entering.

There is a time for everything, a season for every action.

CHAPTER 44: LU

There's nothing special about the water. The water wouldn't change me, wouldn't make me look different, and it would leave no clue. Unless I told them, my family wouldn't know what I'd done when I returned to Dunlap's Creek tonight.

Wouldn't it be great, though, if the water could change a girl – turn the resolutions into reality and make them obvious to all?

That's not how it works, I whispered as I waited.

Grandma Pat had been baptized in the creek. I could see the grain of the overexposed picture I'd included in the anniversary book. The tones told of a hot summer day, and I didn't need to have been there to hear the cicadas. There probably wasn't a fiddle, but I heard that, too, given the bluegrass feel of the occasion – an understated pomp. There was a crowd on the shore, dressed in summer picnic fare, and a line of people in the creek, waiting to be baptized. Grandma was up next, and I noticed her outfit first. Where others had dressed down to get drenched, she'd stepped it up in a full white lawn dress with eyelet embroidery along the neck and sleeves and a large band tied at the waist.

I looked down at the tank top and shorts I'd plucked from my catchall dresser drawer. Grandma would have pushed me to pack something more special or at least something that matched.

That's not the point, I would have told her.

The point was I had packed the clothes at all – in the hope I would put myself in a place where I had to ask and I would ask when the time came. I did it, and I did it here at the church of my crossroads instead of my family's church. This meant Eddy would be the only person who knew me when I stepped in and out of the water this morning, which was fine by me. My anonymity brought privacy to this public act, letting me focus on what I was about to do instead of being concerned with what other people were thinking.

I felt my former self circling me like I was a strange thing.

What are you doing?

Getting baptized.

That doesn't seem like you.

People change.

You're telling me. You used to hate this stuff.

I still do.

Then why do it? Aren't you scared you'll lose yourself?

That's what it's about, I said as the final word to her — at least for this conversation. It was about living my life by giving it back, in faith that God would bring me to myself in a truer way than if I'd held on. It was impossible to understand from where she stood. Some things you have to try.

I stepped in.

"Water is God's gift to us, sustaining our lives here and pointing to the infinite well of God's eternal life," Pastor Eddy said to the congregation. "It also reminds us of the choice we have. Water does no good in a glass next to a parched person. The person has to choose to drink it.

"In love, God created the world. In love, God gave us choice, and we chose to be like him instead of live with him. In love, God gave us another choice. He sent his son, Jesus Christ, to answer for our sins and lead us back to God to live with him forever. His payment opens the way to all who will take it, but it's the only way."

He turned to me.

"Do you believe that?"

I'd meant to go for the quiet nod but instead spoke a loud, "Yes," that earned me a smile from Eddy.

"Then I baptize you, Louisa Marie Sokolowski, in the name of the Father, the Son, and the Holy Spirit."

He braced my back and shoulders, I pinched my nose, and under I went.

CHAPTER 45: LU

Most of the time, life isn't like a book.

But sometimes … sometimes the boy is waiting for you in your driveway.

I knew there'd have to be one more conversation, but I hadn't planned for it to be now. My skin registered the still heat of the night as I left the car and walked to him. I rubbed my arms anyway.

"Jackson," I said, loving the sound of his name on my tongue and hating every word that had to follow. He started to speak, but I held up my hand to stop him. I knew what I needed to say, and I wanted to say it well, but the tears came easier than the words. These, I had to whisper.

"I haven't been honest with you or me. I'm not your friend. I've pretended to be, telling myself it's fine I see you when I see you. I pretend I don't bide my time until the next time, but I do. When I'm with you, I think what I don't have a right to think. I have tried everything I know to move past this, but I can't because I don't really want to. I want …"

I looked down, wiping the tears from my eyes, but more came. What I wanted right now was to leave, but I was almost done. I looked back into his eyes. Green, steady, waiting. *Finish.* I spoke again, stronger.

"I want to be with you, Jackson. Since I can't be, I need to stay away if I'm ever going to have a life in this town for myself."

I turned. I would have walked straight to the front door, but for his hand on my arm. I looked at it.

"How far do you plan on going?"

"Right now? Just inside the house."

"And if I asked you to stay here with me?"

"Did you not hear anything I said?"

"I heard."

"I can't be your friend."

"I don't want you to be my friend."

"Jackson …" I started, but he silenced me by removing his hand from my arm and putting a finger to his lips. He waited until I closed my mouth.

"All day," he said, "All day, and yesterday, and the day before, I've been wondering why two people who want to be together can't figure out how."

He stepped forward.

"I'm talking about you and me, in case you didn't pick up on that."

"What about Rebecca?"

"It's done."

I shook my head. "How long have you …"

"After we danced, you went to the hospital. By the time I got there, you were gone."

"What were you doing?"

"Praying."

"You could have called."

"Some things need to be said in person, Louisa."

"Then, why did you let me go on?"

"It was too good of a speech."

I punched him, and he started laughing. I couldn't stop myself from smiling like a fool. I turned and walked to the deck, but I looked over my shoulder to make sure he was following. When we got there, I crossed to the other side.

"Well?" I asked, raising my eyebrows.

"Well, what?" He was still laughing.

"I'm in person, J. Say what you need to say."

He leaned back against the deck railing and looked at me, his eyes returning everything I felt. The honesty, transparency, vulnerability – the want – it was all there. When he spoke, his voice was low.

"Do you know what I wish? That I'd stopped church the morning you came back and gone straight to you. I wish I'd been clearer before you left for New York. I wish I'd followed. Part of me has wanted to be with you since you told me you smashed your phone with a hammer last summer."

I didn't think he was lying, but that was hard to believe. I shook my head. He continued.

"I can tell you everything about that morning because I notice everything when I'm with you. I feel everything when I'm with you except control over any of it. I keep trying to come at you with my mind, looking for something that makes sense, but if I'm going to be with you, really be with you, I need …"

I don't know when I'd started moving closer, but a fraction separated us now. I rotated my palm to fit in his. His other hand touched my check, and I looked in his eyes, searching for the words he wanted to say. In the end, I wasn't sure whether I found them in him or me.

"You need to let go," I said.

"I need to let go."

Here was the moment. I felt no rush to claim it. First kisses come once. We could take our time.

THE READER'S QUILT

This is the reader's quilt. On this page are the names and stories of those before you who met Lu and felt that her story was one that needed to be shared.

Now, it's your turn. Pick a square, write your name, and the rest is up to you. Jot down some advice. A quote. A story. Color and doodle to your heart's content. Make the square your own. Then, share this book with another. Happy quilting!

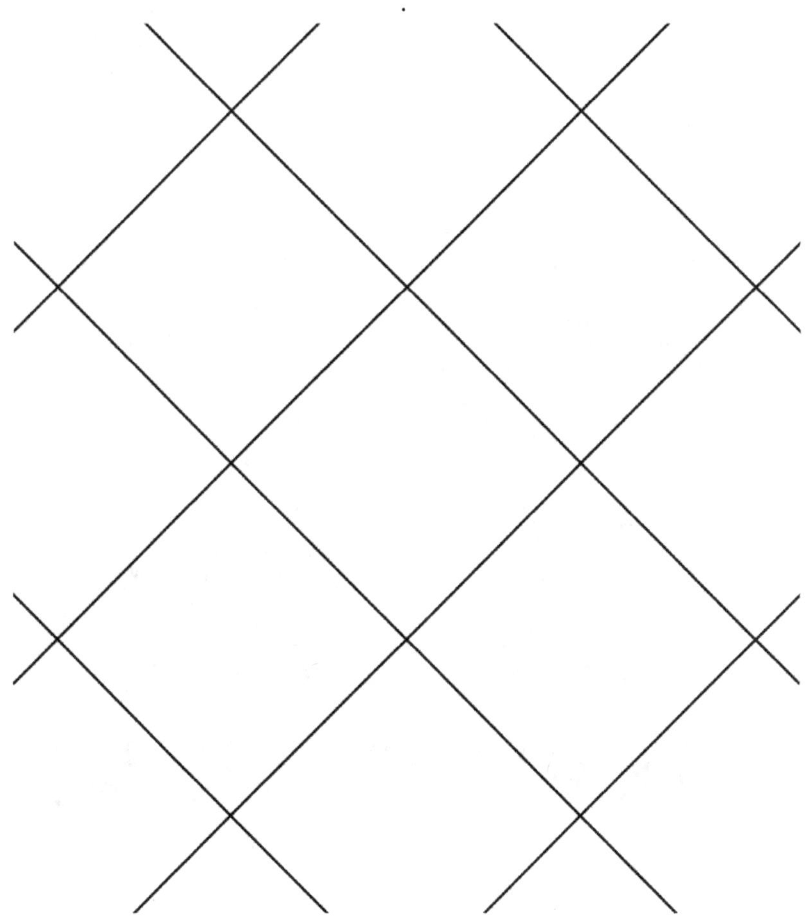

Local Author

GET CONNECTED

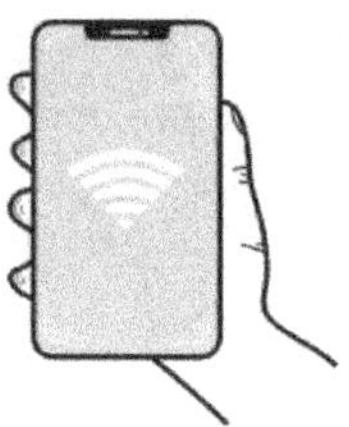

Whether you're there to keep an eye out for updates, comment on their posts, or read their weekly blog, engaging with a local author's online presence is huge. So click that "Follow" button and bookmark that webpage. You never know where it could take you.

Connect with Beth:

@bethtroy.co
www.bethtroy.com

LEAVE A GOOD REVIEW, OR TWO

When you're on Amazon looking for a new yellow throw pillow for your porch bench, where do you look before you purchase? The reviews. Online reviews are important for books too, especially for a self-publishing author. A good review can be the difference between selling 3 copies and 3000 copies. So if you liked the book, say so (and be specific)!

Leave a good review for Louisa:

Amazon
Goodreads

GO SCAVENGING FOR BOOKS

Turn back the clock and go on a scavenger hunt for your local author's novel in a book store. Find it? Turn it face out so the cover can catch the eye of other perusers. Not there? Ask a clerk about it. If they know someone is interested, they just might order it to stock their shelves. More books for you and more sales for your local author!

SPREAD THE NEWS

"Extra! Extra! I really liked this book and you should hear about it!"
Shout your support from the rooftops. Take a #bookselfie and share it with your followers. Post a video book review on your Facebook wall. Talk about a local author with friends and family. Suggest that your book club select a book from a local author for next month's read. Extra time on your hands? Reach out and see how you could help an author promote their brand from behind the scenes.

PASS IT ON

Books are meant to be shared, so why not do so and support a local author at the same time? Give a book as a gift, start a book pass-along (A.K.A. speed dating for books!), invite a few friends over and start a book club, or invite your friend to come with you to a local author's meet & greet. Have fun with it!

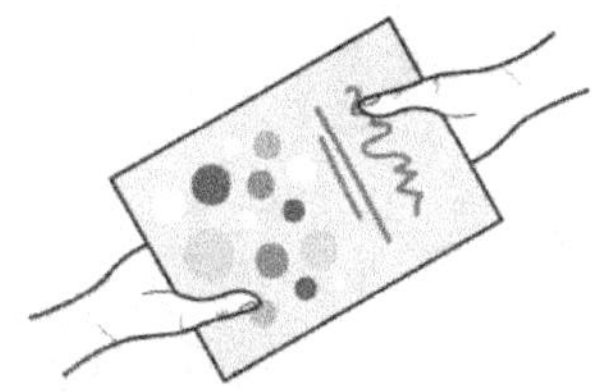

WANT TO GET STARTED?

Meet Beth

Real Woman. Christian. Educator. Mother. Author of Louisa.

Follow her story and send some support her way!

 @bethtroy.co

START AT THE BEGINNING

Are we the sum of our circumstances or is there more? In a debut novel readers are calling "true to life," "captivating," and "cleverly written," author Beth Troy takes on the story of Lu Sokolowski and her life upended. Lu's plans have turned sideways, taking her back to the family and town she always planned to leave.

"This novel is unexpected and revelatory, an example of what Christian fiction can be and do" - *Bookworlder*.

AVAILABLE ON AMAZON

ACKNOWLEDGMENTS

I published my first book to a small circle of family and friends in June 2017. I wasn't sure anyone would come to my book release party, buy the book, or go onto read it. The fact that you read it and requested a sequel still astounds me. Tell me what you want to read next. I am at your disposal.

Publishing a book launched me into a community I never knew existed – a group of dreamers, creators, and entrepreneurs who live out their faith through their work. I want to specifically thank the Ocean network as my gateway into this world where ideas are the currency, risk is the constancy, and faith surrounds it all.

Publishing a book also opened a new conversation with the women around me, one about unleashing ourselves through our work. The one I'm the most honored to lead is Advancing Women in Entrepreneurship (AWE) at Miami University. Ladies, you are my joy. Others can bemoan the future, but I see you. I know what you can do. It will exceed expectation. Now, get to it!

Many thanks also to the crew I worked with in various capacities over the last few years to figure out the business of authoring. Thank you to Peyton Krell and Sam Christie for your attempts to get me in front of a camera, Elizabeth Kilbride for your enthusiasm and social media expertise, Grace Weaver for all things branding (check bethtroy.com for her handiwork!), and Caroline Lunne for serving as my marketing and launch guru.

Which brings me to the Lu + You launch team. Oh, my. My energy was flagging by the time the launch for *Louisa* came around, and your energy sparked mine. Your boldness in sharing picked me back up and saw me through to launch day. Together, we finished the race of this book.

That's the new since *Lu*. Here are the blessed repeats.

Mom! Dad! If you keep peddling my books on the golf course, you're going to get kicked out. I'm not saying stop. Just keep savvy. Thank you for the love and support that fuels the salesmanship.

Laura Smith, my writing partner and foil. Your light pulls me from the broody. I love that I can talk writing with someone and that you are that someone.

Beta readers – Jeni Panhorst, Brenda Homan, Joy Becker, and Mika KariKari. We don't always agree, but you are always right. Even when I'm at my best, it's only 80% of the way there. Thank you for bringing this story to the place readers want it.

My editor, Stephen Parolini. I confess – I did try to sneak some shoddy plot points past you, but you caught them, and in your gentle and wise way, emboldened me to deal with them (I'm talking Chapter 32). Angela Guzman, my copy editor. I never knew how much I used ellipses before you. Thank you for weeding my work. Debbie Freels, a Bible study mate from back in the day and former English teacher who writes her answers in perfect form. Thank you for being the final eye on my proof.

Saturday morning Bible study – Brenda, Christy, and Lara. Your candor, intelligence, grace, and faith is a mix of everything I suspected a group of women could be, but didn't know. I feel more "Beth" with you than I do anywhere, and thank you for accepting me in all of my facets – the times when I can't stay on track, the times when I didn't study what we were supposed to study, the times when I keep talking or asking too many questions, and the times when I'm crying about the same thing I was crying about last week.

And now for the final lap.

God, I humbly submit this book, a meditation of my heart, to you. For years I struggled with where I fit in your kingdom and found your words about losing myself to be terrifying. What if I didn't like who I found on the other side of that loss? Some things we have to walk through. Thank you for love that meets me where I am and refuses to leave me there. Thank you for love that transforms. The other side is beautiful.

My family – Matt, Jesse, Ezra, and Tommy. You know there's nothing glamorous in the life of your resident girl writer. At the end of it, I have little to show that interests you because – again – I didn't include a dragon in the book. Someday (maybe)!

ABOUT THE AUTHOR

Beth Troy is a writer known for her modern take on Christian fiction through stories that portray an intuitive understanding and relevant application of how women today come to know and experience God. Her debut novel, *Lu*, was praised by readers for its wit, relatability, grit, and scriptural depth.

Beth lives in Ohio with her husband and three sons, and she teaches courses in Creativity and Women & Entrepreneurship at Miami University. You can read more about her writing and life at her site: bethtroy.com.